'The Point is top stuff. Engaging from the start, the characters are loveable, the story is strong and the pace never lets up'
Adrian McKinty author of *Fifty Grand*

'What a joy of a novel … The ending is pitch perfect with a Mexican stand off that is Northern Ireland to it's complex core'
Ken Bruen author of *Blitz*

'It needs to be said that Gerard Brennan's The Point is terrific . . . Scorchingly funny, black humour at its finest and the most inventive car theft ever!'
Arlene Hunt author of *The Chosen*

'The Point is the real deal - the writing is razor sharp, the characters engaging, the ending a blast. From start to finish it's true Northern Noir, crafted with style and wit'
Brian McGilloway author of *Little Girl Lost*

'Noir from Norn Iron! A lean slice of grindhouse from Belfast's new crime hack'
Wayne Simmons author of *Drop Dead Gorgeous*

GW00546940

The Point

Gerard Brennan

PULP
PRESS

For more information please visit
www.pulppress.co.uk

First published in Great Britain by Pulp Press

All paper used in the printing of this book has been made from wood grown in managed, sustainable forests.

ISBN-13: 978-1-908544-02-5
Printed and bound in the UK
Pulp Press
12 Little Western Street, Hove, BN3 1AG, UK

Pulp Press titles are distributed by Indepenpress Publishing Limited

A catalogue record of this book is available from the British Library

Cover image: Abigail Horn
Model: Miss Kitty Peels
Cover design: Jacqueline Abromeit

For Michelle, Mya, Jack and Oscar.

Brian Morgan

Brian Morgan woke up in a bath. He wasn't sure whose. His breath stank and his head hurt. The usual hangover from hell.

He patted his shirt pocket. No cigarettes. Just some encrusted vomit. He sighed, wiped his hand on the leg of his jeans then hauled himself out of the bath. With the very tips of his fingers he unbuttoned his shirt and let it drop to the floor.

The kitchen. His brain stuttered to a start as he filled and turned on the kettle. An image of him sinking half-price tequila slammers at The M Club flickered behind his eyes.

Heartburn climbed the walls of Brian's throat. His insides felt as if they'd been scraped out and he'd a gap in his stomach that only fried food and a gallon of sugary tea would fill. Every nerve in his body twanged and his heart raced.

Another mental jolt. He'd chugged beer from a four pint pitcher then performed a hip hop interpretation of an Irish jig on a dancer's podium.

He turned away from the kettle and held his head over the sink. Dry heaved. Wished for a good puke but it didn't come. He ran the cold water and splashed his face. The kettle bubbled, grumbled then clicked. Brian made himself a cuppa, took it into the living room and collapsed onto the sofa.

The early morning sun cut a direct path through the room. Floating dust particles danced in and out of the beam. The golden light bounced a glare off the dead TV screen and threw back his reflection. He wasn't too impressed with it. His unruly hair spiralled out in tangled coils. The dull reflective surface did little for his ghostly complexion.

He reached for the remote control on the arm of the sofa. Found a little note taped to it. It read:

"Hi Brian,

Last night was fun. You were fun. But that's as far as I see it going. Let yourself out when you're ready.

Katie xox"

Brian hauled himself off the sofa. He stuffed the note in his pocket and went to the fireplace. Lifted an ornament then a book as if to examine them for clues. He checked his watch and scooped the telephone from a little table by the door. Then he fished the note back out of his pocket.

"Hiya," Brian said. "She's not here. No. She just left me a note. Told me to let myself out when I wake up and not to bother coming back."

His brother's voice crackled from the other end.

"Did you shag her?"

"No. Maybe. I'm not sure. I woke up in the bath, like."

Brian flopped onto the armchair and flicked on the TV.

He lifted an ashtray from the phone table and rummaged through it for cigarette butts.

Paul Morgan

Paul laughed into his mobile phone as he strutted along the Falls Road. He stopped to light a cigarette one-handed, and took the opportunity to check himself out in a shop window. Winked at his own reflection.

"Ach, for God's sake, wee bro," he said. "That girl was a gift. I knew I should have went for her myself. You always drop the easy ball." He sighed theatrically. "I'll meet you at the flat later, all right?"

Brian let one of his quiet pauses swell. Then; "I'm not sure where I am here, Paul. Might take me a while getting my bearings."

"She lives three streets away from us. You'll find your way."

Paul hung up and used his slender fingers to twiddle with his carefully spiked hair. He was just about to wink at himself again when a shove from behind squashed his face into the window pane.

"What the fuck?" Paul said.

Paul's whole body shimmied from side to side. He dropped his cigarette and struggled against an unknown force. Gasped for air. His face hit the window again. *Oh, Jesus Christ, I'm going to go through this glass.*

The iron grip from a huge hand squeezed down on his neck.

"Get off me, you bastard."

A troll-like voice rumbled in Paul's ear.

"Watch your language."

"You're killing me, man." Paul pulled a breath through his narrowing windpipe. "What's the problem?"

"Mad Mickey wants a word."

"Ah, no." His voice wheezed like a perforated accordion. "What kind of mood is he in?"

"He's mad."

"Ach, shite."

Paul's kidneys seared as he took what felt like a hammer blow to the small of his back. He crumpled to the ground.

"I told you to watch your language."

Paul rolled onto his back and caught a glimpse of a caveman in a suit standing over him. The big guy reached down and flipped Paul onto his stomach then heaved him up by his shirt collar and the waistband of his jeans. Paul was hauled towards a black van parked at the kerb and bundled inside. The van door slammed shut behind him.

The back of the van was carpeted and illuminated by black light and lava lamps. On his hands and knees, Paul could feel the ridges of the van's iron floor under the rough carpet. The worn fibres reeked of spilled bong water. Paul pushed himself onto his knees.

Mad Mickey sat cross-legged on a beanbag. He was dressed in his usual green fatigues and a Rastafarian hat.

Paul licked his lips as Mad Mickey toked hard on a huge joint. Freshened up the stink a little. The forty-year-old hippy with a mean streak exhaled then nodded at Paul.

"Hiya, Mickey. What about you?"

Mad Mickey spoke gently, as if a pain in his throat was bothering him.

"I'm feeling disappointed."

"Sorry to hear that."

"I'm disappointed with you, Paul."

"I'm *very* sorry to hear that."

Mad Mickey stared at Paul. Paul turned his palms up.

"So, why are you disappointed with me, Mickey?"

Mad Mickey heaved a large automatic pistol from a shoulder-holster concealed by his green fatigue jacket. He waggled it at Paul.

"Don't play the innocent, son. It's insulting."

Paul held his hands above his head. He felt a trickle of cold sweat roll down his spine.

"I only borrowed the money, Mickey. I was going to pay you back."

Paul lowered one hand and slowly reached into his pocket. Mad Mickey chambered a round. Paul drew out a brown envelope. He tossed it to Mad Mickey. The hippy-gangster, gun in hand and joint pinched between his lips, opened the flap one-handed, peeked inside and nodded.

"Since you're a family friend, and because you haven't spent any of this, I'll give you a whole week to get out of Belfast." Mad Mickey raised his voice. "Dave. See my friend out, will you?"

The van door squeaked behind Paul as it was yanked open. He almost choked as the suited caveman grabbed him by the collar and dumped him onto the street.

Brother Hoods

Brian had made it back to his own ground floor flat. He half-dozed on his battered sofa, a half-empty bottle of flat cider jammed between his legs. His eyes shuttered open as the doorbell chimed.

"Top of the morning to you, Mr Morgan!"

Brian jolted out of his warm cider-buzz. It was Paul's usual greeting, yelled through the letterbox.

Brian struggled with the warped door, managed to haul it open, and smiled at Paul. "It's afternoon, big bro, but sure..."

Paul's hair sat perfectly in fashionable spikes. Blessed as he was with a tall, lean frame, the older brother made the naff, knock-off Firetrap shirt he wore look good. Brian ran a hand through his own unmanageable mane, and wondered what kind of gel Paul used and why the whole genetics thing was so hit and miss. A few extra inches of height wouldn't have done Brian any harm.

Arms full and straining against the weight of his bounty, Paul pushed past Brian and went straight to the kitchen. Brian stood back as Paul reorganised the scant edible items in the filthy fridge, and filled it up with tins of Carlsberg Special Brew; rocket fuel for the homeless. Brian smiled, even though his stomach lurched a little.

When the beer was tucked away, minus two tins, Brian and Paul sat in the living room and drank warm, syrupy Special Brew.

"I called you hours ago," Brian said "What kept you?"

Paul rubbed the small of his back. "Long story, our fellah. What's the craic with you?"

"Fuck all. Cheers for grabbing the beer and fags."

They banged back a couple of gulps of piss-warm rocket fuel, almost racing.

Paul belched then said: "I need help with a job or two."

"What kind of job?"

"I have to do a few houses over the next few weeks."

"Robbing?"

"No, I mean painting and decorating." Paul crimped his face. "What are you like?"

"I thought we'd agreed to give that shite up. Try and figure out some other angles."

"I know, I know. You want to do victimless crime. Wee insurance scams and all. But they take too long. And I'm not talking about robbing real people. Just a few student houses."

Brian frowned.

"Ach, come on, wee bro! I need to get some funds together. Fast. So, for fuck's sake, can I get an answer today?"

"What's the rush?"

Paul looked around the room. "Look, I've been biting

my tongue for a while now. I just don't think this place is good enough for us. We should move."

"The flat's fine."

"Fuck fine."

"Maybe it could do with a Hoover, but..."

"It could do with a hand grenade."

"We can't afford anything better in Belfast, Paul."

Paul tapped his nose then pointed at Brian. "Exactly! So let's move."

"From Belfast? Where to?"

"Warrenpoint. Remember we used to go there when we were kids?"

"The Point?"

"Yeah, The Point. Remember the ice cream, the amusements, the pier? Ma happy; Da less drunk than usual. Crisps and coke in the pub. Football on the pebble beach. Weren't you always asking Ma for money to windsurf? You could finally have a go at that now. Sure the place was heaven." Paul's face spread slowly in a wide grin. "And, you know, sleepy wee town like that? A couple of sharp Belfast boys could make a penny or two off the local yokels."

Brian drained his beer then crushed the can. He held his tongue and tried to think. The cogs and gears refused to spin. Paul put an arm around his brother's shoulders and led him to the fridge.

"Look," Paul said. "Let's have another drink, and I'll explain why this is the best idea we've ever had."

Rachel O'Hare

Rachel O'Hare took a deep breath. She didn't believe counting to ten was going to calm her down, but she gave it a shot. On the count of seven, she gave up. Her mistake was looking at him while she mentally ticked off the numbers. She should have closed her eyes.

"Sean, drop the scolded puppy look, okay? You don't have the charm needed to pull it off."

"But, Rachel..."

"But, Rachel nothing. We're done. Deal with it."

"Deal with it? We've been going out for months. This is so out of the blue."

Rachel closed her eyes and started counting again. She nibbled on her tongue in an effort to keep it at bay. But then Sean sniffed. One of those big, watery, about-to-cry-me-a-river snuffles. It was too much.

"Out of the blue? I caught you cheating on me, Sean."

She studied his expression in the greenish glow cast by the Toyota Celica's instrument panel. His lower lip jutted and the corners of his mouth drooped. He sniffed again and his face seemed to crumple in on itself. Barely restrained tears glistened in his eyes.

Rachel remained unimpressed. In fact, she was a little disgusted by his weakness.

A shitty chill-out dance mix whispered through the custom sound system. Rachel violently jabbed the standby button.

"Hey, take it easy, Rachel. That's a new radio."

"You weren't so concerned about your precious car when Sheena Magee's stilettos were drumming off the glove box. You didn't even wipe her footprints off it, you stupid eejit."

Sean looked away from her, aiming for a chastised expression.

"Maybe if you didn't keep me waiting," Sean said, "I wouldn't have to go elsewhere."

Big mistake.

"Oh, so it's *my* fault, is it?"

"Well, I'd hardly describe myself as sexually satisfied, you know? I mean, it's been three months. You're a good looking bird and all, but a man has needs and I've never gotten so much as a handjob off you."

Rachel pushed the car's cigarette lighter in. Sean handed her a pack of smokes. She pulled one out, but didn't thank him.

"You have needs? *Needs*? Well, Sean, do you know what I *need*? I need to know that the fellah I'm seeing isn't going to run to some blonde skank every time he feels a bit horny. I need to know that I'm not going to pick up an STD because you can't keep your little willy in your boxers. I need somebody I can trust. And, just for the record, I'd have been happy to drop my knickers months ago. But there's this new concept you might have heard of. Foreplay? Ring any bells? Because I'll tell you something; with your sloppy, lager-tasting kisses, and your clumsy fumbling meat-hooks, you sure as hell weren't ringing my bell."

"That's below the belt." He smirked, squinted a little. There was no humour in the expression.

Rachel felt her lungs constrict. She'd seen that look before. Usually before some poor bastard got the fat end of a pool cue wrapped around their head over a welched bet or spilt pint. He'd not hit her before but she was sure he'd come close to it in the past. Usually when she got lippy with him. Had she gone too far this time? The idea that he might actually swing one of those callused fists at her took hold. The world slowed down.

The lighter popped. Rachel tugged it from its socket.

Aiming for a nipple, she pressed the red hot lighter against Sean's shirt pocket. The heated coils burnt straight through the blue checked fabric and Sean screamed as it made contact with his flesh. He grabbed Rachel's wrist and yanked. She dropped the lighter in his lap. Sean jerked and bounced on his seat. He grabbed the lighter at the wrong end and dropped it again. Whining, he sucked on the burnt fingers of his right hand and managed to snag the plastic knob with his left. He jammed it back in its socket. Eyes wide, he turned to Rachel and took his hand from his mouth.

"What the hell are you at, you mad psycho-bitch?"

Rachel shrugged. "I don't know."

"Get out of the car."

Rachel nodded. "Yeah, I probably shouldn't ask you for a lift home."

She stepped out of the black Celica and eased the door shut. Then she allowed herself a smile. Burning Sean with the lighter was not a nice thing to do. But, God, it'd felt so good. Rachel put Sean and the seafront car park behind her. She wondered if she'd ever meet a decent bloke in Warrenpoint. Her track record with car-loving, townie imbeciles didn't offer much hope.

First Job

Paul's heart raced with anticipation. The time had come. Saturday night, and the brothers were walking around the narrow streets of the Holy Lands. Brian wore a baggy hooded top and an old pair of jeans. Paul had traded in his usual leather reefer jacket for a tatty long overcoat. It covered his knock-off designer labels, instantly gave him that student look he desired and concealed his trusty crowbar. The boys also carried a blue plastic bag each. Each one contained a three litre bottle of cider.

"Cairo Street. Let's do this," Paul said.

Brian just nodded. Paul reckoned nerves were eating at his partner. Good. It'd make him more careful. Paul set the pace and they made their way slowly down the orange-lit street.

It was half an hour until midnight. Paul expected to find most of the houses in the area empty. Cairo Street was pretty run down, which meant forced entry should be easy. Rusty hinges and worn locks were commonplace around these parts. At the weekend, most of the university students went home to their parents. As they got fed and watered for free, Paul was happy to take advantage of the easy targets they'd left behind.

"So, which one?" Brian asked.

"This one." Paul stopped dead in his tracks and turned to his right. He walked up to the front door of number 45 and grabbed the knocker. Then he pummelled the door as if it had spilled his pint.

"What the fuck are you doing?" Brian's voice hissed low but carried a panicked urgency that tickled Paul.

"Relax, son. Expert at work here."

"You're a fucking looper. We'll get lifted."

"For what?" Paul attacked the door again. Brian fidgeted beside him but didn't threaten to run off or ask any more questions. Paul was quite impressed with his little brother so far.

"Nobody home," Paul said. "Follow me."

They sauntered to the bottom of the street and Brian followed Paul into the alleyway that ran along the back of the terrace block. Paul counted under his breath as they passed a number of tall wooden gates set in a dirty brick wall.

"This is the one," Paul said.

"What would you have done if someone answered the door?"

"What do you think the bottles of cider are for?"

"To calm my nerves."

Paul laughed and shook his head. Brian was a hoot, even when he wasn't trying.

"No, you stupid bollocks," Paul said. "If Jimmy Student had answered the door I'd have asked him if the party had started. He'd tell me there was no party and I'd realise I'm on the wrong street, apologise and be on my way. The carry outs are props. It's a new thing I'm trying. Genius, right?"

"And why didn't you explain that earlier?"

"I thought it would be funnier this way."

"Prick."

"Brian?"

"What?"

"It was funnier this way."

Brian shook his head as Paul reached into a ragged slit in the lining of his long coat. He pulled out the black crowbar. Guessing where the deadbolt might be, he pushed the flat end into the gate's frame. Moonlight glinted off the broken shards of glass cemented onto the top of the wall. Climbing was out of the question.

A creak and a snap broke the relative city silence as the old weatherworn wood of the gate gave up and opened. They stepped into the backyard and Paul wrinkled his nose in disgust.

"Look at that pile of bin bags, Brian. These fucking students live like animals. No respect for property at all."

Brian didn't offer his opinion. Instead he closed the gate and wedged some of the black plastic bags against it to stop it from swinging open again. The little improvisation impressed Paul, but he didn't mention it. He wanted to get moving on the next stage. This part was always a lottery. If the occupants had left the key in the opposite side of the door they'd made Paul's life a lot easier. If not, they were stuck. He didn't want to put in the kitchen window and run the risk of being cut to shreds on the way through it.

Paul peered into the keyhole and was disappointed to find it empty. He stood up and kicked the door in frustration. And it swung open. The rotted frame didn't have much fight in it.

"That was cool," Brian said.

Paul nodded and let his brother believe that his good luck was calculated. They entered the house. The kitchen looked no better than the yard. Plates with remnants of food stuck to them were stacked to precarious heights at the edge of the sink. The bin overflowed with pizza boxes and empty beer tins. The stench of sour milk filled the air.

"Tell me this house was abandoned, Paul. I refuse to believe human beings could live like this."

Paul opened the fridge and a new symphony of stink greeted him. He looked at a milk carton on one of the filthy shelves. It had the name Mary written on it.

"This milk is still in date," Paul said. "Someone actually lives here."

"Jesus Christ. Let's get this over with."

Rumbled

The brothers rummaged about in a messy but feminine bedroom. Ruffled pink bedclothes. Bras and panties scattered about. Pretty-boy actors stared down from crinkled posters. Brian moved fast, eager to get the fuck out and start drinking. His big bro didn't seem to feel the same sense of urgency. Paul hooked a pink pair of panties off the floor. He stretched the waistband catapult-style and flicked them at Brian.

"I've met whores with cleaner knickers," Paul said.

"I'm sure you..."

The unmistakable screech of rusted hinges opening cut across Brian's remark. Brian and Paul stiffened with alarm. They stared at each other for a moment.

Brian broke their stasis. "Shit!"

Paul reached into his coat. "Come on. Put this on."

He whipped out a paramilitary-style balaclava and threw it to Brian then pulled down the fold of his woollen balaclava to cover his face.

Brian wrestled with the itchy knitted mask. It smelt musty, interfered with his breathing and itched his skin. Now he could add claustrophobia to the feast of emotions tying his stomach in knots. Paul thundered down the stairs in the loudest possible way.

"Who's there?" A girl's voice. It sounded a little booze-slurred. Brian hoped she was alone.

The girl froze at the bottom of the stairs. She was dressed in Saturday night clubbing gear. Fake tan, short skirt, low-cut top, but most importantly, on her own. She didn't move as Paul clattered into her. Paul cursed and she screamed. Out of instinct, Brian reached down and grabbed her hands to help her up. She kicked up and out. A high heel slammed into Brian's thigh, dangerously close to his balls. He let go of her and stumbled backwards.

"Hey, Mary," Paul said. "Settle yourself."

Mary crab-crawled away from Paul. "Oh Jesus, how do you know my name?"

An easy deduction. The milk told them that somebody in the house was called Mary. The clothes in the wardrobes told them only one girl lived there.

"The IRA knows a lot about you, wee girl," Paul said. "You better stop what you're doing."

"What are you talking about?" she asked.

Brian felt awful. She would piss herself if Paul kept this up.

"Let's go, Max," Brian said. Paul, quick-witted as usual, caught on instantly.

"I told you not to use my real name, Travis," he said. Voice threatening, he turned on Mary. "Don't even think about calling the peelers, Mary. We know where you live."

Paul ran to the front door, yanked it open and, after a quick look up and down the street, pulled off the balaclava and stepped out the door into the night. Brian paused, looked down at Mary and felt powerless. He wanted to comfort her, but had no idea how to do it without making things worse. A few seconds later, he followed Paul out into the night.

Brotherly Love

Paul, no longer wearing his mask, waited for Brian on the footpath outside number 45. Brian stepped out and tugged off his balaclava. His face rippled with a snarl. He stalked towards Paul.

"Not here, bro. We'll talk back at the flat."

"What the hell was that, Paul?"

"Just come on."

At the flat, Paul backed into the living room with his hands raised. Brian shoved him and he fell into the armchair.

"What the fuck was that for?" Paul asked.

"You know what it was for."

"Ach, fuck off. Maybe if she thought the IRA was really watching her she'd make the effort to do a dish or two. You saw the state of that place."

"You were out of order."

"Look, Brian, you can't worry about something like that if we're going to do this. You're not so naive to think that getting robbed wasn't going to upset her, are you?"

"But at least she wouldn't have been worrying about her life being under threat."

"Oh, really? Wake up, Brian. Ninety percent of these students move out after being robbed, to safer, cleaner houses, because they fear a return visit. We probably did her a favour."

"Ninety percent? Did I ever tell you that fifty-seven percent of all statistics are made up on the spot?"

"A joke? Good for you." Paul looked his brother up and down. "Listen, whether you believe it or not, if we rob that place again in a few weeks, there'll be a different name on the milk in the fridge."

"I just think you went too far with the IRA thing, okay?"

"Well, I'm sorry, but I was trying to save you from another kick in the swingers. I'd have thought you'd be grateful."

"She missed my balls."

"Aye, well you didn't give her much of a target."

Brian made a *you're-so-funny* face.

"Look, Brian, I'm trying to help you here, earn you a bit of money. You know I'm looking out for you, don't you? You're my wee bro. The most important person in my life."

Brian stood still. Looked down at his big brother. Paul waited patiently. He was used to his brother's thoughtful gaps. Knew there was no rushing him when he took a moment of quiet.

"Ach, for fuck's sake," Brian said. "Are we going to crack open this cider or what?"

All Apologies

Brian sort of coasted along as Paul dragged him through a cluster of burglaries over five nights. The other jobs passed without any real incident and they ended up with a neat bundle of cash and some phones and laptops Paul's fence would be able to give them a few quid for. He should have been happy. But the girl from the first job niggled at him. Poor Mary. She'd been frightened half to death by Paul's act, and Brian couldn't get her face out of his mind. He had to do something for her, but the best he could come up with seemed so fucking stupid.

Still, it was better than nothing.

He slid a little white envelope through the letterbox in the door of 45, Cairo Street and beat a hasty retreat.

As he bustled down Botanic Avenue he tried to imagine Mary's reaction to what he'd just posted.

***

Mary picks the postcard up from the doormat. The picture on the front is a red-faced cartoon, the word SORRY emblazoned across the top. Mary flips the card over. It says:

"*There was a mix-up. You've nothing to fear from the IRA. The Army Council sends its apologies.*"

Mary looks confused but maybe, just maybe, a little relieved as well.

The Union

Paul and Brian sat at a table under a poster advertising 'Pound-a-Pint' night. A half-full pint stood in front of each of them. Paul thought about how well a couple of half-price tequilas would go down. He tried to wait patiently while Brian studied a list written on a spiral-bound notebook. His attempt was short-lived.

"Those fake student cards were a real money saver. One of your sharper moments, eh, kid?"

Brian glanced up at him, a slight scowl giving away his irritation at being distracted. "Aye, yeah." He glanced down at his list again. "Can you get the loan of a van? I've too much stuff to carry onto a bus to Warrenpoint."

"You won't need that much. The house we're renting is furnished."

"We need a van. If we can't borrow one, they're not that expensive to hire."

"That's a waste of money."

"I don't ask for much, Paul, but I don't want to lug my stuff about on public transport. So think."

Brian took a huge slug from his beer. Paul smiled as a little firework went off in his brain.

"Actually," Paul said. "I do know a man with a van. And he owes me a favour."

"Great. We'll leave as soon as you can get it, then. Okay?"

"Aye, that'd probably be for the best."

A Final Fuck-You

Paul wore a hood and baseball cap. It was a slight deviation from his usually dapper high street attire, but it was a necessary and functional one. He'd been spying on Mad Mickey as the hippy-gangster conducted some business on the street. And, since the hoodie and baseball cap were staples of the Lower Falls dress code, a slight drop in standards made it much easier for him to blend in to the background.

Dave, the suited caveman, leant against the front of Mad Mickey's van and sucked on a cigarette. The faint rumble of the diesel engine told Paul the keys were in the ignition.

Very sloppy, Dave.

Paul used stealth and blind-spots to negotiate his way to the van. He curled his fingers under the door handle and took a heartbeat to compose himself. If he couldn't do this in one fluid motion he was fucked.

You're slick, kid. Just go for it.

Paul jerked open the van door and hopped in. Dave barely had time to register the shift in suspension. Paul cranked it into reverse and Dave toppled as his support was whipped away. Mad Mickey stood, mouth agape, as Paul flew past and gave him the finger.

On the Couch

Rachel rummaged through the magazines scattered across the coffee table. She picked a grubby back issue of *The Ulster Tattler*, a magazine about cars, a current issue of *Chat* and returned to the squeaky waiting room bench. Ah, the Newry and Mourne Health and Social Services Trust. If you were skirting the boundaries of mental health problems, then the fliers and posters tacked to the pastel green walls would transport you direct to Cloud Cuckoo Land. Eating disorders, self-harm, suicidal tendencies; the mines in the field of the delicate young adult psyche.

As always, Rachel's counsellor was running behind schedule. Half an hour past her appointment time and still no sign of life. She flipped through the magazines for another 10 minutes then tossed them back onto the unruly stack of glossies. The receptionist watched her from behind a Perspex panel, eyebrow raised. Rachel tried to make contact.

"Excuse me, is Patrice going to be much longer? Only, if I knew she'd be another half hour I could pop out for a cup of tea and a scone."

The receptionist frowned.

"I could bring you back a scone too," Rachel said.

"Patrice is running a little late."

"Well, yes. That's pretty evident, since I should be on my way home by now. But I'm asking if it's likely that she'll be occupied long enough for me to skip over to The Corn Dolly."

"It's hard to tell," the receptionist said. "And I wouldn't want to interrupt her. Could be harmful for the, um..."

"Patient?"

"Client."

Rachel flashed a saccharine smile. "I'll just wait here then, shall I?"

"Yes, please."

The receptionist nodded and went back to her Marian Keyes novel; *Rachel's Holiday*, of course. *Chance would be a fine thing,* Rachel thought.

For the next 10 minutes, Rachel sat bolt upright with her arms folded and fixed her gaze on the receptionist. Every time the snooty bitch looked up from her paperback, Rachel gave her the crazy eyes. It passed the time. Finally, Patrice bustled into the waiting room and called Rachel's name. Rachel, the only 'client' in the waiting room looked from left to right and then at Patrice.

"Is Rachel O'Hare here?" Patrice asked the waiting masses again.

Rachel waved. "Yes, I'm over here."

Patrice squinted over the rim of her rectangular specs and nodded. "Ah, yes. There you are. Follow me, please, Rachel."

Patrice turned on her sturdy heel and stormed off in a matronly fashion. Very befitting of her physical attributes. Some call it a healthy build. Rachel thought of her as strapping. She could imagine her buxom form squeezed into a mead-stained, low-cut dress designed to keep the medieval patrons of the inn happy. But Patrice was not a serving wench in this life. She was a counsellor. But not just any counsellor: she was the worst counsellor Rachel had ever had the misfortune to meet.

Patrice stood by her desk until Rachel wriggled her bum into the comfy cushioned chair and crossed her ankles. Patrice nodded and settled into her own seat. She leant forward and planted her elbows onto her paper-strewn desk then tented her fingers. Rachel sighed.

"Sorry I kept you waiting, Rachel." It was said as a matter of form with no real conviction.

"Maybe we should make my appointment an hour later next time. Might put you under less pressure."

"Out of the question."

"Yeah?"

"Absolutely."

"Right. Well, it's just that you've been an hour late for my last three appointments. Stands to reason the same will happen again next time."

"Not at all."

Rachel drew her eyebrows together and pursed her lips. She knew it was an immature, petulant expression, but she couldn't help it. Patrice tilted her head.

"So how have we been?"

"*I've* been just peachy, thank you," Rachel said.

"That sounds promising. Any self-harming?"

"What? No."

"You seem surprised that I would ask you."

"Because I've never self-harmed before. Why would I start now?"

Patrice eyed her suspiciously then flipped through her file. "Really? I'm sure I remember an incident involving a Stanley blade."

"There was a Stanley blade incident, but I harmed someone else, not me."

Patrice looked blankly into the space above Rachel's head.

Rachel rolled her eyes. "Fourteen-year-old boy tried to mug me in Warrenpoint with a Stanley knife. I kicked him in the crotch, relieved him of the weapon and slashed his clothes. I broke his skin in a number of places. Nothing deep, but technically GBH and the kid's barrister tried to claim unreasonable force."

"You slashed a 14-year-old?"

"In fairness, he was armed and almost six feet tall. I didn't ask him to produce ID. I just protected myself. Adrenaline sent me a wee bit loopy and I tried to teach him a lesson. He wasn't *hurt* or anything."

"Must have been quite traumatic for him, though."

"*I* was the one getting mugged!"

"Quite."

Rachel took a deep breath. Her temper was slipping her grasp. Of all the places to lose it, a court appointed counselling session was not one of them.

"Have you tried to maim anybody since?"

An image of Sean flashed through her mind. She could almost smell the smouldering shirt. "Isn't maimed a rather strong description? His *scratches* healed without scarring."

"No physical scarring, anyway."

"Are you taking the piss?"

"Please mind your language. We're not on the streets now."

The comfy, cushioned seat no longer felt comfortable to Rachel. She shifted from cheek to cheek then uncrossed and crossed her legs. Patrice watched her through piggish eyes.

"On the streets?"

Patrice shrugged. "Figure of speech."

"Ahem." Rachel checked her watch. "Let's get on with this cra... this session. I want to get out of here as soon as possible. I've already lost my morning. Don't want to kiss my afternoon goodbye as well."

Patrice scribbled something into her pad. "You don't seem to be taking this very seriously."

"I'm sorry you feel that way."

"Are you, though? As far as I can see, you're only here because you have to be. I mean, if I were in your shoes, I'd take advantage of the fact that I have somebody to bounce my problems off. This isn't a punishment, after all. This is a means to rehabilitation."

"Rehabilitation?" Rachel asked. "Yeah, that's great. I can see where you're coming from. Here's the thing, though. I don't really want to be rehabilitated of my natural instinct to stand up for myself. If I hadn't acted aggressively towards my mugger, I could have ended up scarred for life or dead. Seems to me that the law wants me to lie down and take everything these scumbags throw at me. And when they do, they want to run to *them* and offer psychological evaluation? Well, fucking excuse me, but I'm not having that shite." She raised her hand. "And don't tell me to watch my fucking language."

Patrice fumbled with her notepad. She avoided Rachel's gaze.

"So where do we go from here, Patrice?"

"What do you mean?"

"You want to rehabilitate me. I don't want to be rehabilitated. Any chance we can just agree to disagree?"

"Um."

"I mean, we're really not going to get anywhere, are we? Seems to me we're both wasting our time."

"I hear what you're saying, but..."

"Do you, though? I'm not convinced. You had me tagged as a self-harmer earlier. I don't think you have a clue about who I am. How could I ever trust you to help me come to terms with my inner demons when you don't even know what they are?"

Patrice sagged in her seat. It looked as if she'd shrunk a little bit. "I see a lot of clients... I can't be expected to..."

"Every time I come here the waiting room is empty. I'm told your last appointment is running over and you'll soon be with me. Funny thing, though. I never see anybody leave your office before you come and fetch me. Is there a secret passage out of here for your celebrity clients or something? Because I'm beginning to suspect that you're in here napping, or cruising internet chatrooms, or doing yoga, while I waste my time flipping through old magazines and staring at your bitch receptionist."

"Rachel, I really must insist that you lower your voice and calm down."

"Patrice, I really must insist that you tell me the truth. Do you keep me waiting just for the sake of it? Is it some sort of psychological tactic? Or are you just a lazy bitch?"

Rachel knew she had gone too far but she had spent her whole life having her head messed with by social workers and counsellors of varying degrees of competence. After the mugging she'd decided on a zero-tolerance approach to bullshit.

Patrice snatched a Kleenex from the box on her desk and dabbed at her teary, piggy eyes. She cleared her throat, took a deep breath and straightened in her chair. "I think we've done enough for the day."

"That's good, Patrice. I've things to be doing, you know?"

"Quite."

"When's the next appointment, then?"

Patrice flipped through her leather bound diary. "I think you've progressed quite well. I'd suggest we leave the next appointment for about three months. By then, I expect we'll be able to sign off on the court order and your *rehabilitation* will be complete."

"Aces." Rachel stood up. "Any chance you could write me a prescription for some happy pills?"

"I'm not a doctor."

Rachel raised an eyebrow.

"But I can write to your doctor and recommend a course."

"That'd be grand, Patrice. Thanks."

Rachel winked at the receptionist on her way past. Things were looking up.

And They're Off!

Brian drove the Toyota Hiace and Paul drank cider from the bottle in the passenger seat. As a man of modest means, Brian had become accustomed to the smell of alcohol in enclosed spaces, but today it irritated him. The cheap booze smelled like farts and Paul's farts smelt like diarrhoea. He opened the window as they bombed down the fast lane of the M1.

"You don't seem very excited, wee bro," Paul said. "Considering we chose Warrenpoint for you, like."

"I'm just tired. I'll be fine when I get there and have time for a wee drink."

Paul tilted his bottle towards Brian, offering him a sup. Brian wrinkled his nose and shook his head. Paul shrugged.

Less than an hour later and they rolled into a housing estate a million miles away from the built up, redbrick jungles of Belfast. Brian followed the landlord's directions and came to a halt outside a smart semi-detached house. Skateboard's and bikes lay about the house next door's garden. Another house boasted a colourful rockery with seven ceramic dwarfs scattered about it. There was a distinct lack of litter and graffiti.

"Looks pretty good, doesn't it?" Brian said.

"What did I tell you, wee bro? We'll be living like kings, now." Paul twisted the cap back on to his three-quarter-empty bottle of cider. "Want to check out the local pub?"

Brian thought about all the boxes and bags in the back of the van. "Aye. Fuck it. Why not?"

"Sweet."

The Local

"**Here's to me** and my big dick. Fuck everything else. Suck the back of my balls. Amen." Paul's toast boomed across the pub chatter.

He got a kick out of how Brian squirmed and mouthed apologies to the other patrons of *Cearnogs*. He didn't want to stand out yet, but Paul needed to get to work on his reputation right away. He needed to connect, and acting like a loud prick usually got you noticed by the right sort of people; who were, of course, the wrong sort of people.

"Do you want to keep it down, Paul?" Brian said. "At least until the bar fills up a bit and we don't stick out like sore thumbs?"

"You scared of these fucking farmers, little bro? I'm just having a laugh."

"Yeah, well, we're getting the hairy eyeball."

"That's just because we're so fucking handsome."

"Watch the language, Paul. There's kids running about here."

"Well, who the fuck takes their fucking kids to the fucking pub, on a fucking Saturday, at three in the fucking afternoon?"

A barking voice from behind him answered. "I do, dickhead. What of it?"

Paul swivelled on his stool to see a man of about forty, on his feet and angry. A shock of thinning white hair crowned his square head. His craggy, weather-beaten features were tinted red by burst capillaries. He stood a little shorter than Brian but looked twice as wide. Paul thought his longer, wiry arms would give him the advantage over the walrus-necked man. At the table behind him sat a young boy and a slightly older girl. They shoved crisps into their mouths and slurped on tall glasses of cola with lemon slices floating amongst the ice. They looked as at home in the dingy pub as any of the other barflies present. And cool as cucumbers at the prospect of their da getting into a row.

"I think that's a fucking disgrace," Paul said.

"And are you an authority on childcare, pretty boy? You're barely out of nappies yourself."

"Well, I have no formal qualifications, but I don't think I should have to feel guilty about the fact that your kids are listening to my conversation. I should be able to relax with my drink and not worry about impressionable young minds. You're corrupting your children, you stupid bastard."

Brian stood up and stepped away from the table.

"What are you doing?" Paul asked.

"Getting a drink in." Brian looked to the angry local. "Would you like one, mister?"

"No." The local shook his head, momentarily distracted. Then he pointed a finger at Paul. "You watch yourself, son. Next time I see you, I mightn't have the kids with me."

"Let's hope I see you first then."

The local beckoned his kids to follow him and stormed out of the pub. Paul watched after him, smiling. Then he turned to Brian. "'Would you like a drink?' What the fuck, bro?"

Brian shrugged.

"Whatever," Paul said. "I'll get the next round in will I? Do you fancy a wee vodka?"

"It's just after three in the afternoon. You want to hit the hard stuff already?"

"I thought you knew how to drink. You sound like a killjoy girlfriend."

"I'm sticking to the beer." Brian raised his empty pint glass to indicate he wanted more of the same.

Paul half turned on his stool and shouted over his shoulder. "Two double vodkas over here, barman!"

Girls!

The night came fast and the pub filled to the rafters. Brian was relieved to be lost in a crowd. A live band played in a corner. The wall of sound they created prevented Paul's big mouth from getting them in trouble. Things were looking up. The brothers still sat at the same table and were still drinking vodka.

The biggest improvement to their situation was that they were accompanied by two well-suited and booted, carefully made-up, young ladies. Paul had met them at the bar and invited them over. Rachel, dressed to nuke, laughed at some stupid thing Brian had just said. She'd just put him on cloud nine. He didn't even care that Paul was unashamedly eating the face off Rachel's friend, Karen, in plain sight.

Since Rachel seemed to be in giddy humour, Brian pushed the boat out and gave her some observational comedy.

"Ever notice how nobody stands beside each other at the bus stop?"

She licked her luscious lips. "I don't really understand you. You'll have to talk slower."

"Why don't you listen faster?"

"What?"

"Listen faster."

"Oh, right. Very good."

Rachel nodded enthusiastically but Brian got the impression that she didn't understand him.

"You have nice boobs," he said.

"Yeah."

"Me and my brother live in this great house just up the road from here. You want to come home with me? We can have coffee or sandwiches or something. We have a nice bit of ham. You country girls like a nice bit of ham."

"Did you just call me a cunt?"

The horrible word sounded even worse coming from her pretty mouth.

"No," Brian said. "I said country."

"Oh, sorry, you're a little hard to understand. Do you have a speech impediment?"

"Ach, I'm just pissed."

"That's good. I don't like people with speech impediments. They're too much effort to talk to, you know?"

"I think you're a little pissed too."

Then Rachel leaned over the table to kiss him and confirmed Brian's suspicion. She tried to stick her tongue in his eye. It wasn't an entirely unpleasant experience.

Brian and Rachel

Brian always said that there was no way to avoid a hangover, unless you avoided alcohol. He also said that the only thing that made a hangover seem worth it, even at its worst, was the smell of sex in your room and a stranger in your bed.

This morning's hangover had been blessed with both. Blurred flashbacks replayed the drunken, naked fumble in Brian's mind and he smiled.

He pulled open the top drawer of his bedside cabinet and found his breath mints. Fresh breath always increased the chances of a morning shag. When he finished the mint he tried to remember the brown-haired girl's name. He couldn't.

"Hey, sexy," he said. "I've been up for hours, and I'm not talking about being awake."

She opened her eyes to reveal icy blue irises and tried to focus on Brian's face. She didn't seem too disappointed when her pupils adjusted.

"I'm too sick for another shag," she said. "All the bumping and jumping would make me puke."

"Nothing that an Alka Seltzer and a round of dry toast wouldn't cure."

"That sounds like a plan."

Brian knew his Sunday morning sex had just gone out the window. It had to happen before breakfast. The opportunity was usually lost as soon as the girl found her knickers. He shouldn't have offered her anything.

"Have you seen my knickers?" she asked.

"Yeah, they were sexy as hell."

"No, I mean, do you know where they are?"

"I think they're out in the hall. We were caught in a moment of high passion, if I remember correctly."

"You said I wouldn't get pregnant if we did it standing up in the hall."

"I wasn't lying."

"You had a condom and I'm on the pill."

"You can't be too safe."

"You're an eejit."

She sat up in the bed and the blanket fell away from her small but perfect breasts. Her nipples stiffened in the morning chill. Brian's heart fluttered.

"I'll just go get my knickers," she said. "Can I borrow a T-shirt or something? I don't want to give your brother an eyeful."

He pointed to a crumpled heap of cloth on the floor. "Grab that one, sure."

Rachel's side of the bed had been crammed against the wall so she had to climb over Brian to get out. She threw a leg over him and tried to slide-crawl over his body. Her smooth skin was warm and soft against Brian's. Her pubic mound brushed against his erection. Belly to belly she paused, her expression devilish.

"You are so fucking sexy," Brian said.

"You know what? I feel a little better. Maybe breakfast can wait."

Paul and Karen

Paul rooted through Karen's purse. She snored. He thought he was on to a sure thing when he'd taken her to his room the night before. She fell asleep with her nipple in his mouth. Paul would never describe himself as a gentleman, but he wasn't a rapist. He lifted her drunken body from the bed and stretched her out on the floor. He threw his spare blanket on top of her and got himself a good night's sleep.

Just as well really. She didn't look too hot in the morning light. Her lips glistened with drool and her hair sat in a frizzy mess.

Her purse contained thirty-five pounds. He left the fiver in it for her taxi home. Chivalry hadn't quite died.

Feelers

Mad Mickey loitered on his favourite street corner, smoking a spliff. Dave jogged towards him. His cheeks were red and his breath came and went in short puffs.

"Well?" Mickey asked.

"The feelers are out, boss, but no joy yet."

Mad Mickey sucked a long draw off his joint.

"Better get back to it, then, Dave. Right?"

"Aye."

"We're going to get this sleekit wee bastard. And when we do, I'm going to make a bong out of his skull."

"Right, boss."

"Aye. And I'll put his lungs on ice. Might come in handy."

"Good thinking."

"Wonder what kind of hit you could get with a skull bong and four lungs. It'd have to be good, wouldn't it?"

Dave shrugged.

"Are you still here, Dave?" Mad Mickey waved him away. "Go find him, for fuck's sake!"

Rachel Sticks Around

Brian and Rachel had the house to themselves the entire Sunday afternoon. Paul had gone out for a walk after Karen left, to get a feel for Warrenpoint, and hadn't been seen for hours.

They watched some DVDs in the living room, snuggled together on the couch under the duvet dragged off Brian's bed. They ordered a pizza and lazed. They got to know each other better between the action scenes of the Hollywood movies. Complete bliss.

"So, Karen wasn't particularly taken by Paul then?" Brian asked.

"She thought he was okay, last night, but this morning he acted pretty cold towards her. She's a good looking girl and doesn't need to hold on to anyone she's not sure of. Besides, he isn't as sexy as he thinks he is."

"Judging by the amount of girlfriends he's had, I thought he must have been better looking than the Devil himself. I assumed I was missing something or had the wrong idea about what women want."

"But you don't try to be like him?" Her voice didn't brim over with admiration for Brian's choice to be his own person, but it did seem to require an explanation

Brian didn't have one. He did the usual in an uncertain situation. Kept his mouth shut.

Rachel looked at him as if trying to figure him out. Brian gave her a little peck on the lips to mask his discomfort.

"You're even better looking than Karen, but you didn't call a taxi. Are you a little surer about me, or am I just sexier than I think I am?"

"No, I'm just a slut, and I thought if I stuck around a little longer, you'd ride me again."

Her hand found his crotch under the duvet and they christened the sofa while Nicolas Cage and John Travolta chased each other in speed boats on the television screen.

Petrolheads and Cannabis

Paul followed the sound of tuned up engines in his search for a drug dealer. The Point's town centre was small and he'd seen most of it in a 20-minute stroll. Shops, chippies and pubs lined both sides of a wide main street. From both ends of the street a smaller road led to the shore front. Hosting a number of pubs and restaurants, this seemed to be The Point's golden mile. A strong coastal wind shunted him along and he went with it.

A town square mostly served as parking space for the summertime tourists at one end of the town and, on the coastal end, there was an outdoor swimming pool, built on the pebble beach. Paul once heard that the town imported sand from other beaches to take the rough look off the place, but it usually washed away into the sea within weeks. Cider cans and Buckfast bottles added a little class to the attractive seaside scene.

Back on the main street, outside an amusement arcade, a crowd of young men in baseball caps appraised each other's modified coupes and hatchbacks, and revved engines in a show of mechanical strength. Paul could almost smell cannabis burning amongst the exhaust fumes. He'd hit the jackpot.

The lowly drug dealer was usually the quickest backdoor into any gang. A loquacious breed, they liked to impress customers by telling them how well connected they were to the local gangsters. Paul just wanted someone to point out a couple of major players, if a town this small even had more than one, and he would do the rest himself.

A dealer proved easy to find. Paul drifted over to the car with the most teenagers flocked around it and jumped into the back.

"What the fuck are you at?" the skinny man in the driver seat asked. He turned with a jittery energy, probably unsure if he was being attacked or set up for a prank. He looked a bit younger than Paul and ugly as sin. His adolescent acne had not completely given up the war on his pockmarked face.

"Well, spotty, I want to buy some drugs." Paul gave the dealer his best cheesy grin.

The dealer laughed and looked out the rolled down window at his next customer.

"Come back in five minutes, boy," he said to his chubby, young customer. "I need to have a chat with this old mate of mine."

He rolled up the window of his tricked-out car and turned again to face Paul.

"Way to save face," Paul said. "Pretend you know me. I'm impressed."

"Fuck off," the skinny dealer said.

"Hey now, there's no need to be like that. I just wanted to introduce myself."

"Well hurry up and introduce yourself. Then fuck off. I have customers waiting here."

"What's your name, mate?"

He puffed his pigeon chest. "John O'Hare. Do you want to know what my favourite colour is too?"

"Don't get stressed, John. I'm new in town and just wanted to make a new contact. My name's Paul, by the way. Now, sell us a bit of dope, will you? Being the new kid is very stressful."

When John handed Paul the little brown block he nodded at the back passenger side door. "There's the exit, Paul."

"Look, you seem to be a sound guy. How about I skin up here and we share a spliff? Call it a goodwill gesture."

Of course, no self-respecting drug dealer ever turned down a free toke. Paul and John were soon nattering away like a pair of long lost sisters.

Impressions

"Top of the morning to you, Mr Morgan!" Rachel jolted in Brian's arms as Paul's voice boomed from the letterbox. Brian gave her a squeeze of reassurance. He sighed at the interruption. For a few hours their whole world was the sofa and the television. The yelled salutation had been a rude awakening.

"It's only Paul."

"Loud bastard, isn't he?"

"I guess."

Brian leant in for a kiss. She pushed him away and he got up to answer the front door.

"You live here, Paul," Brian said as he opened the door. "You could just use your key."

"I forgot it."

"How do you forget your key?"

"I've never needed one before now. It's not something I naturally reach for when I'm leaving a house."

"Yeah, but you didn't try and lift the TV as you left either. I guess that's half the battle. Well done."

"Nobody likes a smartarse." Paul noticed Rachel. "Oh, you're still here."

"Charming," Rachel said.

Paul giggled. "Sorry, I didn't mean it like that. I'm just surprised this loser hasn't scared you off yet."

Brian sat on the sofa, beside Rachel, and Paul flopped onto one of the two armchairs. The glow from the television screen lit up his red-rimmed, half-lidded eyes. Brian took note of his dopey grin.

"Where'd you get the hash, Paul?"

"Who says I have hash?"

"I know what you look like when you're stoned."

Paul raised his hands. "Okay, you got me." He spoke in a woeful gangster accent. "I found a dealer down at the arcade opposite the supermarket."

"Slots-o-Fun?" Brian asked.

"That's the one. Skinny, spotty guy in a done up Citroen Saxo. Sound as a pound he was."

"Was his name John, by any chance?" Rachel asked.

"Aye, how'd you know that? Is he your dealer too?"

"No, he's my brother, and the wee shite told me he had no gear last night. I'll kick his hole when I see him."

"Oops, guess he lied to you. What a coincidence, though."

"That is weird, isn't it?" Brian said.

"No," Rachel said. "It's just a small town."

"Aye, it is," Paul said. "Here, he invited me to a party at his place. You two want to come with me?"

"To my own brother's house? As much as I appreciate the invitation, I'm happy enough here."

Paul turned to Brian. A sardonic smile played on his lips. "She's calling the shots a bit soon, isn't she?"

"Play nice, Paul."

"I'm just messing. Are you sure you don't want to come? Wee John was raving about this coke he got a hold of from some Newry crew."

"You know I'm not a chemical head. But you go enjoy yourself, right?"

Paul jumped out of the armchair and threw his arms in the air. "PARTY!"

When he left, Rachel said: "I'm sorry, but your brother's a prick."

"Ach, he's just stoned."

"Whatever." She shook her head as if to dismiss Paul from her mind. "So what's the deal, anyway? You two sticking around The Point for a while?"

"Aye, it's nice here. I can't see us flying off any time soon."

"You could probably use a job, then."

Brian shrugged. "Could I?"

"Well, I don't shag dole moles."

"Guess I should get a job, then. What kind of work is there around here?"

"It just so happens, I know a man who could help you with that."

"Who?"

"My daddy."

Working Man

Brian stood at the bottom of a staircase leading from the shop floor to the offices of Malone Industries. His first interview in years was due to commence. He'd been instructed by the floor supervisor to stand there and wait a while until the bossman, Barry Malone, was ready for him.

After a sweaty-palmed five minute wait, Malone tramped slowly down the steel industrial stairs. Brian swallowed hard as he placed him as the man Paul had fucked with at the pub on their first day in town. Brian backed off a little as Malone practically stood on his toes and glared at him.

"Uh, hi. I'm Brian." It was the best he could come up with.

"I know. I've seen you before, haven't I?"

"Um..."

Malone clicked his fingers. "Yeah, I remember you." He jabbed Brian's chest with a thick, callused finger. "Lucky you didn't give me any cheek that day, or you'd be picking a lump of timber out of your hole."

"Right. Look, I'm..."

Malone held his hand up to silence Brian. "You got a bad back?"

"No."

"You know how to count?"

"Yes."

"Does your alarm clock work?"

"Yes."

"Start tomorrow."

Malone held his hand out and Brian shook it.

"Your hands are too soft, son. But we'll sort that out soon enough."

That following night, Brian sat at the kitchen table, picking splinters out of his fingers. He cursed each one as he sucked, bit and pinched at them. Paul stood at the kitchen sink and watched him, then pulled a quarter bottle of gut-rot whiskey from a kitchen cupboard. He handed it to Brian.

"Be a man. Suffer in drunkenness."

Brian smiled in gratitude and took a slug from the bottle.

"They're looking for more labourers at the mill. Do you want me to put a word in for you?"

Paul looked at Brian like he'd pissed on his shoes.

"You're not exactly an appealing advertisement for the place. I'm all right for now, wee bro."

"But you are going to look for a job, aren't you?"

"We'll see. Jesus, man. Take it easy, okay? Life's a marathon, not a sprint."

"So what are you going to do for money?"

"Don't worry, wee bro. I'm working on it."

Networking

While Brian busted his hole dragging wood around the saw mill, Paul networked.

Paul had never dealt drugs. He'd never even so much as sold a spliff to a mate for the price of a pint. He had no qualms with smoking weed or necking the odd E, but he knew that dealers were usually complete wankers. He wasn't sure if that was just the personality type that took up the profession, or if it was something you had to develop to become successful in the field. Either way, he didn't feel cut out for it. He considered stealing more honourable. And more fun.

Nevertheless, he risked guilt by association and rode around with John in his little Citroen as he did laps of the town on weeknights, and sat with him when he parked outside Slots-o-Fun or in the town square at weekends. The drug dealer/wanker rule was particularly well illustrated in John, but Paul put up with it.

On one of their laps, John had pointed out a teenaged Goth-type dragging his clunky boots across the town square.

"See him? That scruffy wee bastard stiffed me for a 10-deal last month. I gave him credit for the first time and I haven't seen him since. I'm going to have to knock him about a bit. Can't have him telling his freakshow mates I'm a soft touch."

Paul thought John had a bit of a cheek, commenting on someone else's appearance, but he kept that to himself. "Well, if you want, I'll get the money off him."

John gave him a hopeful smile. "Yeah?" Obviously, he wasn't keen on the violent side of the business.

"Aye. Park here and come with me."

They hopped out of the Saxo and tracked the teenager at an inconspicuous distance. He led them to a little cul-de-sac halfway up the Bridle Loanan Road. They broke into a sprint as the young fellah fished his keys out of his knee-length leather jacket. The wee Goth jerked to attention at the sound of their trainers pounding the tarmac. He stood wide-eyed, like a stunned cliché caught in HGV headlights. Paul grabbed him by the lapels and shook him.

"Pay John what you owe him or I'm going to get your ma out of bed and tell her you smoke dope."

The Goth opened and closed his mouth, at a loss for words. Paul shook him again.

"Ten seconds, wee lad."

"I... I... don't have any cash on me."

"That a fact?" Paul said.

"Seriously, I don't. But I've a bit in my room. I can go get it."

"No. We're not stupid," Paul said. He glanced at John. "Well, *I'm* not stupid. You've probably got a big knife up there for sacrificing chickens and whatnot. No chance I'm letting you go in and get it. Empty your pockets."

The teenager had a snazzy Samsung mp3 player and a top of the line Nokia mobile phone on him. Paul handed John the phone and pocketed the wee Samsung sound-box.

"Ach, lads," the kid protested. "I don't owe anywhere near that much. It was only an aul' 10-deal."

"Sorry, wee lad," Paul said. "But you have to factor in interest, late payment charges, and then there's my finder's fee. It all adds up, son."

"But they were Christmas presents."

"Now, to be fair, I'm sure they warned you in school that this sort of thing would happen if you got caught up in drugs. Welcome to the dark side, wee man."

Paul ruffled the kid's long, black hair and smiled encouragingly.

"Nice doing business with you," John said, like any wanker would.

The kid disappeared into his house and Paul and John set off back to the square.

"Paul, that was great," John said. "Too funny." He shook his head and chuckled. "Listen, I'm going to do you a favour. Point you in the direction of a real player around these parts. What do you say?"

"Sweet."

The Big Boy

Paul thumbed through a newspaper at his table in the corner while he enjoyed an ice-cold lager. John sat beside him, fidgeting and flipping beer mats. Bennett's was a small pub, even by Warrenpoint's standards, but it seemed pretty clean and they took care of the details. A very attractive barmaid stopped by regularly and wiped away the wet rings his glass left on the table. She smiled at him each time. Paul imagined what she would look like naked: hardly a huge stretch of the imagination. Her short skirt and unbuttoned polo shirt gave him a good start. He filled in the blanks with ease.

A big man entered the bar and spoiled Paul's view. This guy's slow gait could best be described as a lumber. This was a word Paul had come across in books when the urge was in him to read, but he'd never actually seen it in action. The man's walk, combined with his pure white hair, made Paul think of the clinically depressed polar bear that had died in Belfast Zoo a few years back. An expensive suit jacket stretched tight across his shoulders. John gave Paul a sharp nudge in the ribs.

"That's him," John said.

"Oh, yeah?"

"Aye. Richard O'Rourke. Alleged car dealer. Uses his garage as a front for an illegal car smuggling trade. He started out as a mechanic, but look at his hands. Clean. They haven't touched an engine in years."

"Fuck me," Paul said. "He could squish my head in one of those fists."

"So don't give him reason to."

"You going to introduce me, then?"

"Fuck, no. I'm scared shitless of him. But you're the one keeps nattering about going big-time. O'Rourke's the man to talk to."

Paul felt like strangling John but, instead, he nodded and got out of his seat. The three pints he'd downed while waiting for O'Rourke to show up set him at ease. He walked up to the bar and winked again at the sexy wee barmaid.

"Could I have another pint, please? And get this man whatever he wants."

The barmaid looked to O'Rourke and raised her shapely eyebrows.

O'Rourke didn't even glance at Paul but was happy to accept the drink.

"Double brandy."

She smiled, nodded and got busy fixing the drinks.

"It's Mister O'Rourke, isn't it?"

His big boulder of a head swivelled on its elephantine neck. He locked on to Paul with a thousand-yard stare. "Until I know you better, son."

"I'm Paul. You look like a man who can't pass up

a good business opportunity. Will you hear me out for a second or two?"

O'Rourke's suddenly focussed glare conveyed that he wasn't mad about the idea. But, because he didn't outright say so, Paul gave him the pitch after the barmaid set down their drinks and disappeared out back.

"I think I might be able to supply you with some good quality used cars. I moved down here from Belfast a couple of weeks ago. I've a few contacts in the city and a lot of relevant experience. I think we could help each other out. You don't have to decide right now, I'm sure you just want to relax after a day's work. But, if you have a business card with you, perhaps I could call you during office hours tomorrow?"

"I'm a businessman, son," O'Rourke said. "Every hour is an office hour."

"That's my philosophy too. I hope it brings me as much success as it seems to have brought you."

O'Rourke shrugged off the compliment with a snort. Paul made a mental note. The man was not impressed by arse-lickers.

"Right," Paul said. "This is how I can see things working for us. I'll call you once a week and you'll give me a wish-list of cars. I'll bring you everything I can from it, as soon as I can, and you decide if the motors are up to scratch. I propose we start small. One or two cars to begin with and we'll see where it takes us."

O'Rourke adopted the same approach to conversation as he did to movement; slow, steady and economical. When the barmaid was out of earshot he answered Paul.

"What makes you think I'd be interested in that kind of business, officer...?"

"I'm not a peeler, Mister O'Rourke," Paul said. "And I've done my homework. Eddie Matthews from Twinbrook says hello. You can phone him for a reference."

O'Rourke gave Paul the hairy eyeball. Paul held his ground and O'Rourke's gaze. Eventually, O'Rourke nodded.

"Okay." Even O'Rourke's whispers rumbled. "I assume that they'll be basic ringers. A changed number plate as a temporary fix with the serial numbers intact, right? I can move these out of the country but the overheads are high. We won't be talking about big money."

"You can quote a price before I search out the car. That way I can assess the risk better."

O'Rourke handed Paul a card.

"Call me tomorrow and I'll give you your first job."

And, as easy as that, Paul had branched out.

Coffee and Scones

Rachel hid her girlish grin behind her coffee cup. Too late. Karen had caught it and latched on mercilessly.

"You're smitten!" Karen said.

"Ach, don't be ridiculous. I've only just met him."

"Oh my God, you're blushing!"

"Shush you, I am not."

"You are!"

Rachel sighed. She *was* blushing. And she suspected that she was a wee bit smitten. She couldn't think about Brian without a dopey grin creeping across her face. Talk about soppiness.

Karen pulled a lump off her blueberry muffin and popped it into her mouth. She chewed quickly and rinsed it down with a sip of tea. She looked from left to right, checking the proximity of their table for earwigs then leant forward in her cushy chair. Her voice was almost drowned out by the café's customer chatter, but Rachel had pretty much guessed what the question would be, so she'd no trouble picking it up.

"Have you slept with him yet?"

Rachel fought back the dopey grin as it wrestled for dominance again. She nodded.

"You wee slapper!" Karen said, a little less concerned by her volume.

"Keep your voice down."

"When?"

Rachel grimaced. "On the first night."

"The night you met him?"

She nodded again.

"You dirty stop-out."

"Hey, take it easy, you."

They smiled at each other and fell silent. Sipping on their beverages, they took turns to shake their heads and roll their eyes. Karen had called Rachel that morning to let her know she was in town on company business and had an hour to spare around lunchtime. Rachel was in the mood for a good chat, so she'd arranged to take a long lunch and met her chum at the little coffee shop on Church Street. Talking about Brian lent reality to the dreamlike dizziness of their stupidly intense affair. She'd never known herself to give so much to a relationship so quickly. It was exciting and scary at the same time.

The bell above the café door tinkled. Karen sat facing it and her eyes widened slightly as she glanced over Rachel's shoulder.

"Um, I think that guy you used to go out with just walked in."

Rachel froze. *Oh, God. Don't let it be Sean.*

"It's Sean," Karen said.

Rachel found a spot on the table and fixed it with a fascinated stare. She wished for a paper bag to pull over her head. But there was nowhere to hide, especially not in a small town like Warrenpoint. Sean towered over their table and cleared his throat.

"Hi, Sean," Karen said.

"How're you, Karen?" Sean paused for a couple of seconds. "Are you not talking to me, Rachel?"

Rachel finally looked at her ex. His expression was unreadable. Cold and emotionless. She shrugged. "It'd probably be best if we didn't talk at all, Sean. I don't think either of us have anything to gain from each other's company."

"I see. So you think you can just brush me off?" His voice was deadpan, and still his face betrayed no feeling.

"I'm not brushing you off. I'm just... I... There's no point in us trying to be civil to each other. We parted on bad terms. We're only going to stoke the ill feeling between us."

"Bad terms? Is that how you describe it? More like sadistic, perverted assault, if you ask me."

"Look, I know Sheena's a bit of a boot, but I think that's an unfair..."

"I was talking about you trying to burn the tit off me, you psycho-bitch!" His face instantly contorted as he spat his words through bared teeth. "If I had a cup of battery acid right now, I'd throw it in your face!"

"Sean!" Karen said.

"Karen, don't," Rachel said. "You shouldn't get mixed up in this."

Sean didn't even register Karen's protest. He seemed to be doing his best to burn holes in Rachel with his mad, glaring eyes.

Rachel realised that every customer in the café had turned their attention to the unfolding drama. She'd never be able to show her face in the place again. And it wasn't as if the town was coming down with nice coffee shops.

"Get lost, Sean. You're making a show of yourself."

"You're a dirty, skanky bitch, Rachel O'Hare!" He'd bent at the waist so he could get right in her face.

"And you need to brush your teeth, Sean."

A couple of patrons laughed nervously. One or two hissed in anticipation of Sean going nuclear.

"Hey, you!" The clear voice boomed through the heated atmosphere. "What are you at?"

A man in a white apron stood at the café's counter. Rachel guessed he'd been summoned from the kitchen by the nervous waiting staff. He wasn't big, but he had that little hard-man look about him. All sinewy muscle and intimidating stare. Sean stood up straight and turned his attention to the new player.

Rachel couldn't help herself. She fired a punch into Sean's groin. Then another. And another. He squeaked and folded over. The men in the café groaned and crossed their legs in unison. Sean fell onto his side and curled into the foetal position. Karen screamed.

"We should get out of here, Karen," Rachel said and dropped a twenty pound note on the table. She turned to the man in the apron. "Sorry about the commotion. Keep the change."

She stepped over Sean, who she almost felt sorry for, but he made a half-hearted attempt to kick out at her and she caught herself on. She booted his rubbery leg away and hunkered down so she could make sure he heard her through the pain.

"How was that for a handjob?" she asked.

You Dirty Rat

Paul stood at the traffic lights on the main street in Warrenpoint with a cardboard box at his feet. He spotted a red Audi TT convertible with the top down approaching. It wasn't the first time he'd seen it scooting around the town's streets. The little blonde driver must have been based in one of the small offices in the town but had a job that took her out and about. Or, more likely, she was a trophy wife who had little else to do all day but burn petrol as she went about a handful of unnecessary tasks to put in her day. Paul had a very keen eye for pretty motors and he'd clocked this one's routine for the last couple of days.

He pushed the button for the pedestrian crossing. The lights changed on cue and the car slowed to a stop. Paul winked at the blonde trophy wife driving the car. She licked her lips and smiled at him. He pulled a humane rat trap out of the cardboard box. There was a live rat inside, scratching at the plastic bars. Paul opened the trap and dumped the rat onto the passenger seat. The trophy wife screamed and clambered out of the car, scrabbling over the door instead of opening it. It was a less than graceful exit. Paul grinned, threw the trap into the passenger side foot-well and hopped into the driver's seat. He peeled off.

"Okay, Mister Rat, thanks for the help. Now just you crawl back into your wee house there and I'll drop you off at the shore with a big block of cheese, deal?"

The rat hopped onto Paul's lap. Paul screamed.

Fast Track Promotion

Paul raked the TT's engine as he sped into O'Rourke's remote lock-up. One of the young mechanics had to dive to the side to avoid certain death. Paul didn't bother with the car door, but vaulted out over it and performed a disjointed dance by the side of the vehicle. He ignored the puzzled stares from O'Rourke and his two young engine-heads as he gave himself a full body search.

O'Rourke's voice rumbled slow and calm. "What the fuck are you doing, Paul?"

"I hate rats." Paul continued to dance but edged away from the Audi.

"Okay. But what's that got to do with the price of chips?"

"I've just driven six miles with fucking vermin as a passenger. It kind of freaked me out, okay?"

O'Rourke ambled over to the car and looked in. He grunted and bent over the door as he reached inside. The adult brown rat squirmed in his huge, powerful hand. The rat's struggle became a frenzy of jerks and squeaks. Its tiny bones crumbled as O'Rourke clenched his fist. One of the mechanics screamed as the rat's stomach split and a loop of its purplish intestines sprang out like a popped watch spring. Paul fought the urge to vomit. He had embarrassed himself enough already.

O'Rourke threw the rat's carcass into a rusty barrel full of old oil. He looked Paul up and down.

"Why was there a rat in my beautiful sports car, Paul?"

"It's a long story."

O'Rourke shrugged. Paul shuddered.

"Okay then, Mister O'Rourke," Paul said. "That was the last car on your list. Have I proved my worth yet, or are you going to send me off on another test raid?"

"Paul, you've impressed me. I didn't expect you to complete our little probationary period so fast. Until I get these ones shifted I won't need any more cars. I'm running out of space to be honest. But I do want to give you some more work."

"I'll do anything that won't get me killed, Mr O'Rourke."

"Good." O'Rourke cracked a rare smile. "And, by the way, you don't have to call me Mister O'Rourke anymore. We're friends now. Call me Richard."

Paul nodded and smiled. O'Rourke offered Paul his slab of a hand; the hand that had crushed the rat; the hand that he hadn't washed the rat's blood from; the hand that could easily crush Paul's windpipe if he ever fucked with the big bastard. Paul shook his boss's meat-hook and kept his poker face on. The grip was slimy and slick with rodent gore. O'Rourke pumped hard, jarring Paul's arm in its socket. Paul did his best to relax his muscles and hoped his arm would remain attached to his body.

O'Rourke released Paul's hand to answer his mobile. Saved by the ringtone. Paul wiped his hand on the arse of his jeans and allowed himself the luxury of a skeleton rattling shudder. What a way to seal a deal.

The L Word

Brian and Rachel lay on the sofa in each other's arms, gasping. They untangled from each other and grinned like loons. Brian snuck a hand down to his crotch and adjusted his thrumming dick. Rachel patted the pink skin of her chest and tried to steady her breathing. Brian admired the jiggle of her pert boobs that each pat set off. The sound of Rachel's tummy rumbling sent a hunger pang ricocheting around his gut.

"We should go for a meal, babe."

"What, now?"

"Yeah, why not? I'm sure we'd get a table at the wee pizza place on the shore front. It always looks empty."

"There's probably a good reason for that, Brian."

"Well it isn't about the food when you're young and in love. It's about the company." He'd said the 'L' word before his brain had filtered it. His post-orgasm mind allowed it through. He hoped she hadn't noticed.

"You said the L word."

"Shit."

"Do you love me?" Rachel's hopeful expression

made it impossible to lie to her or make a joke out of it.

"I love you, babe. It's only been a few weeks, I know, but, Jesus, I just can't stop thinking about you when you're not around, and pinching myself when you are. I love the way you laugh and smile and move, and when you get naked... mother of God, I can't control myself." He couldn't stop the words from spilling out of his mouth. He prayed that she'd say something back, if only to interrupt him before he started to quote Shakespearean sonnets.

"I think I get the picture, Brian."

"And?"

"And I love you too, you big eejit. But if you mess me about, I'll cut your balls off."

Brian stared at her in wonder and she stared back. For at least a minute he struggled to come up with something to say. In the end he settled for, "cool."

"Let's just order a pizza in," Rachel said. "I'm in the mood for an early night."

She slid a soft hand down Brian's spine and cupped one of his buttocks. Brian felt the first twinge of a fresh hard-on.

"Cool," he said.

Mettle Test

Paul perched himself on the radiator outside O'Rourke's office. There was nothing as grand as a waiting area in the grotty wee building at the back of the garage. He stood in a widened hallway with just enough room for a small, cluttered desk and a thin receptionist/secretary/PA. Paul had been summoned to the office via a phone call from one of the underlings. Possibly the mechanic he'd almost run down in the TT. He didn't know him well enough to be sure, but there'd been a hint of aggression in the abrupt message.

Oil pervaded the entire hallway. Oily footprints on the floor; oily handprints on the office door and dotted along the white-painted walls; the smell of oil in the air. Paul's slightly dodgy stomach flip-flopped and his grim surroundings offered little relief. So, he checked out the pretty receptionist/secretary/PA in an effort to ignore his nerves. Black hair with red streaks. Low-cut white V-neck T-shirt. Decent cleavage. False tan, but closer to brown than orange. She wasn't bad for a Warrenpoint skank. He cleared his throat and tried to catch her eye.

She smiled at him. "Mr O'Rourke should be ready for you very soon."

"Thank you, um...?"

"Bernice."

"Bernice. That's a nice name."

"Ah, no. It's common as muck."

"Really? I've never met one. Apart from you, like."

"You're not from around here, though. There were three Bernices in my class at secondary school."

"I bet you were the best looking one."

She blushed just a little bit. Hard to detect under her spray-tan, but Paul was looking for it. He was in there.

"You're a bit of a charmer, are you, Belfast boy?"

"It's Paul, and no, I don't think so. I just reckon you'd be hard to beat in the looks department, you know?"

"Well, it just so happens, you're right. The other two were complete dogs." She put a carefully manicured hand to her lips and giggled. It was a pretty, feminine flourish.

"So what do you like to do with your time when you're not working, Bernice?"

"Ach, you know. The usual. I like to get out for a drink and a bit of a dance when I can get a babysitter."

Paul's interest in Bernice took a sudden dive, but he didn't let the Mister Smooth act falter. He didn't want to piss her off. She probably held a bit of sway with O'Rourke. Especially if she'd ever shagged the big bastard.

"Oh, you've got a kid? Boy or girl?"

"Little girl."

"She's not called Bernice, is she?"

She smiled at him, delighted he was taking an interest.

"No, she's called Natasha."

"Ach, like a wee Russian doll."

"Right enough, yeah."

He nodded for a bit and waited for another conversational gambit to occur. She filled the gap.

"Have you no kids, yourself?"

None that I know of, he thought. "No, haven't met the right girl yet, you know?"

"Oh, waiting for Miss Right? Very romantic."

"Aye, I'm straight out of a chick flick, so I am."

A static crackle cut through their flirting. They both jumped a little.

"Send him in." It was O'Rourke speaking through a cheap intercom, brief and brisk as per.

Bernice rolled her eyes then pushed a button on the little speaker. "Okey dokey, Richard," she said in a sing-song voice.

Paul gave her a little wave and strode into the office. O'Rourke sat in his high-backed leather office chair; a heap of beef and gristle. He nodded slightly and pointed to a visitor's chair. They had company. As he sat, he noticed the other guest was bound and gagged.

"What the fuck is this?" Paul asked.

"Meet Charlie," O'Rourke said.

Charlie stared at Paul with pleading bug-eyes. Sweat and tears streaked his bloody face. Paul shook his head and looked to O'Rourke for an explanation. O'Rourke raised a big, meaty finger to his lips, then used it to click on the intercom.

"Bernice, take yourself out for a long lunch today. You've been working very hard this week. Lift twenty quid out of the petty cash tin and have a treat on me."

"Ah, thanks, Richard. You're a real sweetie."

He grunted, flicked off the intercom and waited until the clip-clop of Bernice's departing heels faded into the distance.

"You want a beer, Paul?" O'Rourke asked.

Paul wanted to get the hell out of the office but, since running away was likely to be considered bad form, he nodded for the beer. O'Rourke reached down to his side and Paul heard the rustle of a plastic bag. The big man straightened and plonked a six-pack of Harp lager onto his desktop. He peeled one from its plastic ring and tossed it to Paul, who caught, cracked open and chugged it. Paul wiped his sleeve across his lips and burped into his fist.

"Thanks. Lovely and cold."

O'Rourke nodded and smirked. "I'd say Charlie would enjoy one too."

Charlie shook his head.

O'Rourke tugged another tin from the pack. "I insist, Charlie."

Charlie jerked in his bindings and managed to move the chair a fraction of an inch. Very little payoff for what looked like a shitload of effort. His ribcage rose and dropped like a sewing machine needle as he fought to regain his breath. Paul wanted to tell him to relax, but it wouldn't do Charlie any good and he doubted it would have impressed O'Rourke. He took another swig of beer.

O'Rourke launched the beer tin at Charlie. It bounced

off the poor fucker's forehead. Paul managed to stop himself spraying his own beer over O'Rourke's desk. Charlie made little keening noises, muffled by the cloth gag. O'Rourke rumbled a sadistic laugh and pulled another beer.

"You dropped that one, Charlie. Must try harder," O'Rourke said.

The next tin thumped off Charlie's chest. Paul winced. Charlie hitched for breath. O'Rourke grinned. He pulled another tin. Charlie croaked guttural protests from the back of his throat and hummed through his nose. He blinked wildly to clear his eyes. A huge lump had already formed across his forehead. Paul squirmed and sweated. O'Rourke cracked open the tin and gulped greedily from it.

"What the fuck is this?" Paul asked, struggling to steady his voice.

"Bit intense for you, Paul?"

Paul looked to Charlie again. He'd stopped struggling against the ropes and cable-ties. His eyes were closed and his breathing slowed. A bloody mucus bubble expanded and contracted in his nostril.

Paul shrugged. "Depends what he did, I suppose."

"Ten out of ten, Paul. Good man."

Thank God, Paul thought. *And, Jesus, please keep me out of that chair.*

Charlie's nose-bubble popped as he snuffed a deep breath and coughed into his gag. Paul was sure he would choke but poor Charlie managed to clear his airway and swallow whatever had clogged it.

"So what did he do?"

"Charlie here has run up a bit of a debt. He's a gambler who never learned when to hold or fold 'em."

"Big money?"

"Very big. And he's been avoiding me for a few months now. Couldn't let it go on."

Paul shifted in his seat and cleared his throat. "You, um... you going to kill him?"

O'Rourke chuckled; the dry rumble of a boulder rolled from a tomb entrance. "I haven't decided. On one hand, killing him means writing off a bad debt. But it also sends out a strong message to other weasels with bad ideas brewing." He narrowed his eyes. "Why don't you decide, Paul?"

"What?"

"You decide. Should Charlie here live or die?"

Paul tilted his beer to his lips and took a slow sip. His mind raced. Obviously, O'Rourke had hauled him in here to test his mettle, but killing some poor bastard with a gambling problem? It was too hardcore. Paul decided straight out that he wouldn't suggest Charlie die. What he needed to do was come up with a good reason to keep the guy alive. He set his tin between his legs and resisted the urge to rub his sweaty palms on his T-shirt. *Be cool, be cool, be cool.*

"Here's the thing," Paul said, impressed that he spoke without squeaking. "There's no real gain for you if Charlie dies. Like you said, a dead Charlie is a bad debt written off. You also said killing him sends out a strong message. I disagree. Who's going to spread this message? Me? Don't think so. At this stage I'm implicated in the murder, so blabbing about it will only get me scooped. You're not going to chat about it either, are you? Will Charlie? Not unless he goes through a medium."

O'Rourke pinned Paul to his seat with a steady, unflinching gaze.

Paul continued. "So let him go this time, under the proviso that for every additional week he avoids payment, you're taking a toe, then a finger, then an ankle... you get where I'm going, like."

"I'd say Charlie will be very grateful that you're arguing his corner," O'Rourke said.

"Arguing his corner? Pfft. Fuck that. I'm looking out for *you*. This Charlie fellah doesn't mean anything to me. He's just some eejit who got himself into a mess."

"Really?"

Paul stood slowly. He turned in a half-circle and threw a kick from his hip. His shin crashed into Charlie's chest. Charlie toppled backwards in his chair and cracked the back of his head on O'Rourke's carpeted floor. Paul rounded the toppled heap and soccer-kicked Charlie's skull. He pulled it slightly on contact, but Charlie's unconscious head whipped to the side. Paul spat on him.

"When he wakes up, tell him he'll get a lot worse if he runs to the cops on either of us."

"I'll do that, Paul."

"Did you want me for anything else, Mister O'Rourke?"

"I told you. Call me Richard."

"Anything else, Richard?"

"No, Paul. I'll call you later. I've some new addresses for you. Bigger payers."

Another raise, Paul thought. "Okay, Richard. That'll do well."

Paul gave poor Charlie another glance on the way out. His chest rose and fell steadily. Paul kept the relief from his face. *You're lucky I'm a clever bastard, Charlie. Very lucky.*

A Lead

Mad Mickey shifted his arse cheeks but it did no good. He just couldn't find a comfortable spot on the wall in front of the house on his favourite corner. It was too cold, too hard, too high. He missed his van. Couldn't wait until he got it back. Until then, he'd have to put up with pins and needles in his hole.

Big Dave sucked hard on a fag as he ambled up to Mad Mickey. He looked like he might be smiling though, in fairness, it was hard to tell. With the big wide jaw and sloping forehead, Dave was a man who always looked angry, even at the best of times.

"They found your van," Dave said.

"Yeah, where?"

"Just outside Newry."

"So we know where he is, then."

"Well, we know he's somewhere near Newry. He'll not have burned it in his own back garden, though."

Mad Mickey lit a spliff. "He burned it?"

"Afraid so."

"Fucker." Mad Mickey puffed on his joint and held the smoke in his lungs until it burned. He coughed out a cloud of brownish-bluish smoke. "Okay, it's a start.

Get in touch with anybody who owes us a favour in the surrounding towns. We'll catch him yet."

And then I'll set fire to his balls.

The Chinese Connection

The bell above the door sounded a gentle ping as Paul pushed it open. A friendly face greeted them at the counter of the Welcome Inn Oriental takeaway. The man was Chinese but his accent pure Belfast. Paul hoped he wasn't an Antrim Road Triad. Brian followed behind Paul. He slurped on a huge ice cream cone he'd bought on the way to the takeaway.

"Can I help you?"

"I'm here to pick up something for Mr O'Rourke."

"Who?"

Paul sighed for dramatic effect and pulled a piece of paper from his coat pocket. He unfolded it slowly and cleared his throat before he read from it.

"The Welcome Inn Oriental Takeaway, collect six-hundred quid from Jimmy Ching."

"Oh, *that* Mr O'Rourke?" Ching said. "I told him to fuck off last month. I have my own protection. I don't need his."

"Look mate," Paul said. "You're on the list, pay the fucking money and let me get on my way."

"Get out of my establishment." He reached under the counter and pulled back a meat cleaver. In one swift motion he sank it into the counter top with a deep thud. His hand disappeared again and came back with another one. "I have a blade for each of your heads."

Paul and Ching locked into a stare. He didn't think the guy was bluffing. He'd kill the two of them without a second thought. Paul's mind went blank but he didn't break eye contact. Inspiration would have to hit him soon.

Then, Brian stepped past Paul and threw his ice cream. It hit Ching in the face, blinding and distracting him. He dropped his cleaver as his hands went to his face.

Paul vaulted the counter, stood on the dropped cleaver and pushed Ching backwards. Ching slammed into the wall. Paul could see Brian climb over the counter in his peripheral. Brian grunted as he yanked the first cleaver from the counter top. He tapped Paul's shoulder and Paul turned to be greeted by a death stare from his little brother. Paul shrugged and returned his attention to Ching.

"You should probably hand over the money, mate, or me and my partner will get to work on you with these cleavers."

The shell-shocked man pointed towards the till. Paul hit the sale button and the drawer popped open. He slowly, deliberately counted six-hundred from the pile of twenties. This done, with a smile, he scooped out two-hundred in ten pound notes.

"I'm taking a little extra for the trouble you caused, mate. Next time, just hand over the money."

The Chinese man nodded and waved them away. He'd been bluffing. They'd scared the poor guy shitless.

Paul was relieved to see it. It meant less chance of a comeback. The guy had a cracking poker face but no backbone. He screamed when Paul raised the cleaver and faked an attack.

Brian fidgeted awkwardly at Paul's side, not at home in the situation.

"Where's your CCTV video?" Paul asked.

Ching pointed to a shelf under the counter. Paul ejected the tape and pocketed it.

The bell above the door pinged as they left.

Brian pulled ahead of Paul with a jerky strut. The older brother had to jog to catch up. He grabbed him by the elbow on the corner of the block and dragged him to a halt.

"Jesus, bro," Paul said. "That was brilliant! You're the man! You moved like lightning there. Where did that come from?"

Brian screwed up his face like he was still trying to figure out what had just happened. "I threw my ice cream at him," he said.

"What can I say, bro? I'll buy you another one."

"Another one? No. That's not..."

"But can you see now how you're made for this shit?"

Brian's confused expression gave way to a snarl. He grabbed a handful of Paul's shirt and pulled him close.

"No, I am not made for this. I feel sick. Why didn't you tell me you were there to collect, you fucking wanker?"

Paul held his hands up. Brian let go of Paul's shirt and rubbed his stomach. He hesitated before speaking again.

"You know, when you said we were going straight, I believed you. What kind of a mug am I?"

"Ach, come on, bro. You don't really want to lift wood for the rest of your life, do you?"

"Why not? It's an honest job. And I'm making more money off that than I ever did robbing houses. It's stress free and I feel good about myself. So fuck you. I don't want to follow your lead anymore."

"Follow my lead? What are you talking about? We're partners."

"The fuck we are. I've always been your lackey; your back up. Fuck that shite. You'll get me banged up or killed, you selfish fuck."

"What's got into you? That bitch, Rachel? You letting some skank get between us?"

"Call her a skank again. See what happens."

"Why? You in love?" He smirked at Brian then panicked when he didn't respond. "Wait. She's not up the duff, is she?"

Brian spat at Paul's feet. "Fuck you, bro."

Brian marched away. Paul yelled after him: "Come on, wee bro. Is she pregnant or what?"

Brian marched on.

Ex, Bogs and Rock and Roll

Brian nodded his head in time to the bass drum. Headrush, a local band, cranked out a killer Thin Lizzy riff with gusto. The singer sounded nothing like Phil Lynott, but he rocked the vocal line in his own way. A cigarette-ravaged blues whisper that scaled octaves like a Sherpa skipping up the Mourne Mountains. The guitars were tight and the drummer mean. Brian could feel the bass line in his ribcage. The semi-pro musicians really took themselves seriously around these parts, and these guys worked extra hard.

Brian and Rachel sat in a booth with an excellent view of the slightly raised platform the five piece band had been crammed on to. They were completely at ease in their adopted local bar, *Cearnogs*. Brian, who'd failed Irish language along with most of his other GCSEs, had asked Rachel what the bar's name translated into. She'd rolled her eyes and smiled. "It doesn't mean anything, babe. The owner just thought it sounded Irish."

Whatever the origins of the name, Brian enjoyed his surroundings. He buzzed on a feel-good high. Every so often Rachel squeezed his hand. Conversation was impossible in the all-consuming noise, but that was okay too. They were forced to sit quiet, enjoy the drink and soak up the vibe-fest of tunes.

Rachel was the cool kind of chick that insisted on buying her share of the drinks on a night out. She even went to the bar to order them herself. And when the band took its break it was her round. He watched her denim-encased backside sway as she cut through the crowds to reach the bar. She made his heart go giddy-up.

While he waited for Rachel, he scanned the pub and he noticed a tough-looking guy at another table giving him the hairy eyeball. Brian nodded at him. The gesture wasn't returned. The guy just continued to stare.

Rachel arrived back in record time and blocked Brian's view of the eyeballer. She clunked two whiskey tumblers onto the table. Then she picked a rolled up scrap of paper from her mouth and waved it at Brian.

"That pretty wee barmaid gave me her number!" she said.

"Seriously?" Thoughts of the eyeballer were instantly shunted aside. "I notice you took it."

"Yeah. I thought we could maybe see if she'd be into a threesome."

"Really?"

"Sure. I'd have to try her out on my own a few times, though. Would you mind? I mean, it's not cheating if I tell you about it."

Brian could actually feel his inner conflict plough furrows across his forehead.

Rachel laughed. "I'm messing with you. Jesus. You're too easy."

Brian shook his head but smiled a little.

"So she didn't give you her number?"

"Oh, she did. I just took it to be polite, though. Still, she's a stunner isn't she? Good to know I appeal to more than one demographic."

Brian raised his glass and waited for Rachel to do the same.

"To demographics and hot lesbians."

Rachel winked at him. "*Sláinte!*"

They threw back their drinks. Brian sucked in a deep breath and whooped as the slow burn warmed his chest from the inside out. Rachel took hers like a seasoned pro.

"Powerful," Brian said. "Here, babe. Do you know that guy over there? The grumpy-looking fellah in the pinstriped shirt?"

Brian jutted his chin towards the eyeballer and, sure enough, the guy was looking back at them. Brian caught his eye and nodded to him, but he looked away and took a sip from his bottle of beer.

"Ah, shit." Rachel said.

And then it all became clear. "Ah. He's an ex, then."

"Yeah. That's Sean."

"Think he'd try to start something?"

Rachel shook her head, but didn't look entirely convinced.

"Well," Brian said, "if he wants trouble, I'll handle it. Don't worry."

Rachel gave him a look. She knew fine well that Brian was no fighter.

Sean moved off out of sight a few seconds later. There was a tangible sense of relief at the table. The night was going well and they both wanted it to continue that way.

The band came off their break and kicked off with a sizzling version of Sabbath's *War Pigs* that had Brian bouncing on his seat. Possibly a little too much bouncing. As the track ended he made his way to the gents.

The urinals were all occupied so he took a stall. He emptied his bladder with a long, luxurious stream that seemed to come from his toes. Then, because he felt like being nice, he closed the lid and flushed. He'd just tugged his fly shut and turned when the boy in the pinstriped shirt from the bar stepped into his path. Brian evaluated him: a little taller; a little broader; a lot drunker. The urinal-hoggers had left and they were alone.

"Can I help you...?"

"We need to talk, boy," Sean said.

"No we don't, Sean." Brian held up placatory hands. "I'm having a great night, and I don't want any silly business messing it up."

Sean got right up into Brian's face. Then he ripped open his shirt to reveal an ugly burn just above his nipple. A perfect circle about the size of a ten pence piece with a crusty green layer of scab. Brian wrinkled his nose.

"Rachel's insane," Sean said.

"That's disgusting, mate. You need help."

"No, you do, Curly Bap. Rachel did this to me!"

Then the door to the toilets swung open and suddenly Sean was sent flying, almost knocking Brian over.

Faster than Brian could react, Paul pounded Sean into the cubicle door. It juddered open and Paul rammed him into the cubicle. The impact cracked the toilet roll dispenser. Sean shrieked.

Paul slapped him about. "What's your problem, mate?"

"What the fuck?" Brian said. "Jesus, Paul. Wait, it's all right."

Sean, dazed and confused, tried to salvage some pride. "I'll kill you, you square-headed Frankie bastard."

Paul kicked Sean between the legs. As Sean bent forward, Paul punched the side of his head. The townie went down and stayed down.

"Paul!"

Paul looked at Brian. "What?"

"Jesus, this is some day. Between this and the Chinese I'm choking on an ulcer here." He rubbed his stomach. "Have you not traumatised me enough today?"

"What can I say, bro? He was right up in your face. I thought I was looking out for you."

Brian frowned. Paul chuckled and glanced at Sean's prone figure.

"And what the fuck were you doing here, anyway, Paul?"

"I was lurking at the bar, trying to work up the nerve to come over and apologise for earlier. I got worried when I spotted that header follow you in here."

"Oh." Brian didn't know what else to say.

"He was melting your head, wasn't he?" Paul said.

"Aye, he was. But I don't think he was going to hit me, like."

"Better safe than sorry. Let's go get a drink, eh?"

"Yeah, just wait a second."

"Why?"

"I haven't washed my hands yet." Brian looked from Sean to Paul. "You should wash yours, too."

Round Table Meeting

Rachel linked arms with Brian, craving his body heat in the midnight chill. Paul hung back with some slapper he'd picked up at last orders. The dirty bitch was welcome to the creep. At least she'd keep him occupied and away from her and Brian.

"Wasn't that a cracker of a night?" Brian said.

"Yeah, it was class," she said.

"And it's not over yet."

Normally, Rachel wasn't one for all-night partying, but she was caught up in Brian's party-boy energy. It was contagious. Brian's eyes gleamed feral in the orange fluorescent street-glow as he smiled wildly. His unkempt curls added to his animalistic image. She wondered if he would ever straighten up and fly right, but wasn't sure if she wanted him to. The undomesticated thing was half the appeal.

"Here, Brian!"

Paul's loud Belfast twang stopped Rachel and Brian in their tracks.

"What?" Brian said.

"I could eat a horse. We should get something to eat."

Rachel had a sudden craving pang. "I'd love a chicken

chow mein. Can we go to the Welcome Inn?" Brian and Paul exchanged a glance.

"What did I say?" Rachel asked.

Paul sniggered in the way that always made her skin crawl.

"Ask Brian," he said.

"Brian?"

"Um... Paul just knows how I feel about Chinese food. Bit of a poisoning incident a few months ago, you know?"

"Yeah," Paul said. "One of those double-ended projectile deals. Horrible."

"Yuck!" Paul's slapper said.

"Fuck's sake, bro. I don't think Rachel needs the details."

"All right, boys," Rachel said. "I think we can move off the topic. Anybody got a problem with pizza?"

They didn't, and pretty soon after they were seated around the kitchen table at the boys' house, washing down mouthfuls of double pepperoni with vodka and Coke. Rachel ate as voraciously as the boys, and within 10 minutes of silent munching, they'd reduced the late night feast to so many pizza crusts.

Brian sat back and rubbed his belly. "God, what a feed."

Paul took control of the vodka bottle and poured them all a drink to place himself in the leadership role, as per usual. Rachel was on to all of his wee tricks.

"How's the job going, wee bro?" Paul asked.

Brian spoke in a careful, almost stilted way as he

answered. "Good, thanks. I keep picking up the wood and they keep paying me."

"It'd be hard enough graft, I'd say."

Brian nodded.

"My daddy says he's a brilliant worker," Rachel said. "He even thanked me for setting up the interview."

Brian sat up a little in his chair. "Did he?"

"Yeah, he did. He sees potential in you."

Paul sneered. "Potential? What as?"

Rachel narrowed her eyes. She'd seen enough of Paul to know when he was leading her in to something.

"Somebody who could work his way up. From floor supervisor to management, if he puts the effort in."

"Ach, he'll never make any real cash in a dead end job like that. No offence, like, bro."

"Pfft! None taken, Paul," Brian said.

"And what would you have him do?" Rachel asked.

"I'm already in with Richard O'Rourke. With a couple more lads behind me and Brian as my lieutenant, we could be running things on the ground. O'Rourke's getting on in years. He'll want to take a step back from the hands-on side of the business soon. Me and my crew would be there to fill the void."

"So, that's your career plan, is it?" Rachel asked. "Gopher to the mighty Richard O'Rourke. Wow, you're such an entrepreneur!"

"Oh, my ambitions stretch way beyond that, wee girl. But we all have to start somewhere. And at least in my job I'm not risking limbs pushing big whacks of wood towards hungry saws."

Paul topped up the glasses as he spoke. Brian gave him the stink-eye. Rachel approved.

"I'm just saying, Brian," Paul said. "You're street smart, and you've got balls. You're not destined to be a working stiff. You're too good for it."

"I don't want to talk about it." Brian said.

Paul turned his palms up. "Okay, Brian. Okay. I'll mind my own business. But I just want you to know, if I could choose anybody to watch my back, it'd be you."

"Whatever. Just fill me up, will you?" Brian waved his empty glass at Paul.

"Okay, we're out of Coke, though."

"I should be all right."

Rachel cringed at the sight of Brian drinking straight vodka in enthusiastic gulps. Brian barely flickered an eyelid. Rachel found a couple of beers at the back of the fridge and shared them with Paul's slapper while the brothers got stuck into the neat vodka.

The mood dulled and the conversation morphed into a slurred, drunken commentary on movies and society. When the vodka bottle emptied, Paul kissed, groped and spanked his slapper all the way to his bedroom. Rachel was delighted to see the back of them. She just hoped it wouldn't be a noisy, porn-style marathon. Her stomach wouldn't be able to take it. Brian filled two pint glasses with water and Rachel lit two cigarettes double-barrel style. They smoked and sipped tap water in bleary-eyed contentment.

"Your ex cornered me in the bogs at *Cearnogs* tonight." Brian said.

"What? Why didn't you say? Did he try to hurt you?"

"I didn't want to bring down the mood. And no, he didn't try to hurt me. Though Paul jumped to the same conclusion, to Sean's, um... misfortune."

She struggled to focus on Brian's face and pay attention to him. "What did he do, then?"

"He kicked his balls and punched him in the head. Left him there. Sleeping it off, like." Brian lent his elbow on the table. It slipped off the edge as he tried to prop his head up with his palm. He giggled.

"Paul kicked Sean?"

"Yeah. Misunderstanding, though. We felt wick about it, and all."

"Well, maybe he'll learn. Third time's a charm. But I meant, what did Sean do? Not Paul."

"Oh. Oh, right." Brian blinked, one eye at a time, and smiled. "At first I thought he was coming on to me. He ripped open his shirt."

"Oh, God. He wanted to show you his chest."

"So you did do it, then?"

Rachel took a deep breath. She studied the glow of her cigarette then snuffed air through her nose. "Did I burn him with a car cigarette lighter? Yeah. But I'd a good reason."

"A car lighter. Ouch." He looked at her through one squinting eye. "Why'd you do that?"

"I don't want to talk about it."

Brian flicked ash off the end of his cigarette. It landed a good four inches away from the ashtray. He nodded. "That's fair enough. I don't usually pry into people's past but, you know, when a guy flashes his maimed boob at me, I get curious."

"So, you must think I'm a psycho, then."

"I think you're fucking fantastic. That's all that matters."

And he leaned in to kiss her. It was a drunken, sloppy, drink-stinky, smoky, pepperoni-tasting kiss. Their teeth scraped together and somehow, the end of her nose got wet.

But it was fucking fantastic.

Hardware

Paul rarely admitted to himself that he was capable of real fear. He liked the idea that he was afraid of no man. Impossible to ruffle. But as he sat opposite Richard O'Rourke, ridiculously aware that his balls had shrunk to the size of raisins, he had no choice but to face the simple fact; Richard O'Rourke was the scariest man on the planet and Paul had just asked him for one hell of a favour.

O'Rourke shifted forward in his seat. The solid mahogany desk creaked beneath his elbows. To Paul, O'Rourke's head looked like an oncoming meteor. The kind that destroys worlds.

O'Rourke cleared his throat. "And you want a gun because...?"

Paul straightened in his chair, tilted his head back and faked his usually natural confidence. "That Chinese guy got the drop on me. I thought all your clients knew the score and just paid up but, if one was willing to take a chance, who knows? Maybe the next time I won't be so lucky."

"And what if you get lifted by the cops with a gun on you?"

"I'll risk it."

"But will I? What's to stop you selling me down the river?"

"Come on, man. I saw what you did to Charlie. Think I'd be that stupid?"

"Maybe."

Paul sighed. "So you're telling me I can't have one?"

"No."

O'Rourke opened a drawer in his desk and pulled out a revolver. He set it on the desktop. Paul eyed it.

"I'm telling you not to get caught with it," O'Rourke said. "If you do, I'll kill you."

Paul nodded.

O'Rourke went on: "This is a .38 snub-nose. Very reliable piece, and easy to conceal. But you should keep in mind that now I know you have this, I'll be thinking of you as one of my soldiers rather than one of my thieves. There's a lot attached to that."

Paul nodded solemnly and reached for the gun. He weighed it in his hand and checked out the sight. Then he looked at O'Rourke.

"Thanks for this, Richard. Could I ask for one more favour, though?"

"Depends what it is."

"Can you show me how to load it and all?"

Meet the Parent

Brian felt a certain comfort in the weight of the blue plastic bag he carried. Nothing beats a substantial amount of alcohol in a blue bag to keep you calm in a social situation. But it wasn't quite enough to get him through the next stage in his relationship with the girl of his dreams. As he stood at the door of Barry Malone's... *mansion* he reached a hand out to snag Rachel's. She gave it a little squeeze.

"Are you nervous?" Rachel asked.

"Yes. Is it too early to drink?"

"At my dad's place, it's never too early."

"I'll probably be all right after a couple, then."

"Okay, but don't get too wasted. If you come on to my step-mother my daddy will probably kill you."

"Step-mother?"

"Yeah. I'll tell you all about it some day but, so you know the basics, my mummy's not around these days and daddy's started a new family with a new wife. We don't mention our John, so you can't either."

"Why can't I mention...?"

"Shush. Daddy's coming."

Malone opened the front door. He greeted Rachel with a hug and Brian with a brief smile, then led them in.

Guns Kill People

John's little Citroen Saxo wobbled on its lowered suspension as a gust of coastal wind hammered the passenger side. Paul still felt edgy after his meeting with O'Rourke and almost yelped as the car rocked in its parking space. John didn't notice, though. He was too transfixed with the little revolver in his hands. He turned it this way and that, studying it from all angles. Practically drooled. Then he raised it up and pointed it towards the windscreen. Paul reached across and pushed John's arm back down to keep the weapon out of sight, all too wary of the number of pedestrians cutting through the car park.

"And he just gave it to you?" John asked.

"Aye."

"Fuck. That's class. You're pure gangster now."

Paul shrugged. "I suppose so."

"Have you field tested it yet?"

"What, like target practice?"

"No, like shoving it in somebody's face. That'd be class."

"Are you wise? Guns aren't fun, okay? They kill people."

"People kill people."

"Ach, fuck up, John."

Paul grabbed the gun by the barrel. John resisted giving it up.

"Wait," John said. "Can I borrow it?"

"What for?"

"I noticed a sign in Murdock's garage earlier. The chip and pin machine's broke. No credit cards. People have been paying cash for fuel and shit all day long."

"No way. Not a chance. Too fucking risky."

"I'll be taking the risk. You're taking twenty percent."

Paul relaxed a little. Felt his interest pique at the thought of some easy cash.

"Twenty-five."

John smiled. "We'll call it thirty. But you're the wheels-man."

Kitchen Nightmare

Brian tried to settle into Malone's leather couch. It squeaked and creaked with each buttock shift. Sweat soaked his boxers. He didn't get the attraction. Rachel perched herself beside him, pretty and elegant. He imagined how he must look to Malone in contrast. Brian wished he'd gotten around to visiting the barber and ran his hand through his tangled hair. It didn't make it all the way through and he had to withdraw.

"Is Becky not coming?" Rachel asked.

Malone shook his head. "No. She took Catherine and Liam to the cinema."

Rachel turned to Brian. "That's daddy's other family."

Brian smiled through his awkwardness and discomfort. He wished Rachel wouldn't push her da's buttons in front of him. Brian had no idea how to react to it. It made things 10 times worse that Malone was Brian's boss as well.

Malone seemed nonplussed, though. "I haven't offered you two a drink yet, have I? Sorry. I'm a bit distracted."

"Aren't you always?" Rachel said.

Brian stood and thrust out the blue plastic bag. "Some wine." He despaired at his monosyllabic speech and general jerkiness and the bag began to weigh on his straightened arm. He gritted his teeth and held it steady.

Malone looked at the bulging bag and smirked. "Some?"

"Aye. Sorry. I didn't know what kind to get and they were doing three for a tenner. So, I got six different ones. Sorry."

"Don't apologise, Brian. That's very generous. Three for a tenner, too. Good deal."

Brian nodded. Malone nodded. Rachel cleared her throat.

"Daddy?"

"Yes?"

"Do you want to go open a bottle or something?"

"Oh, yeah. Right. Back in a minute."

Malone hurried off with the wine and Brian sat back down. He balanced rigidly on the edge of the couch. Rachel rubbed his back.

"You okay?" she asked.

Brian scrunched up his face. "Nope. This is no craic at all. Can we just leave or something?"

"Do you not think that'd be a bit rude?"

"I don't know. Would it?"

"Yes it would. Just chill, okay?" She fiddled with a length of her hair then said: "Did daddy seem a little distant to you?"

"No. He was right there. All big and ready to punch me in the face and all."

"Catch yourself on. No, he seemed kind of out of it. I wonder what's going on."

Brian shrugged. He had his own problems.

"Can you smell burning?" Rachel asked.

Brian sniffed and nodded. Rachel grabbed him by the arm.

"Come on 'til we see what's going on," she said.

Rachel led Brian to Malone's kitchen. They found Malone scooting from one corner of the room to the other. Smoke uncurled from an open oven door. A smoke alarm went off and Malone grabbed a tea towel. He waved it under the alarm, trying to clear the air around it. Brian clocked a half-empty bottle of wine on the kitchen table.

"Daddy, such an effort," Rachel said. "You shouldn't have bothered... Really."

Malone jumped as he noticed Brian and Rachel in the room for the first time. The smoke alarm stopped bleating. The sudden silence sent a wave of relief through Brian's body that un-bunched the muscles in his shoulders. Malone shuffled on the spot, embarrassed.

"Yeah, sorry," Malone said. "There's been a bit of a kitchen incident. I ruined the roast." He tossed Rachel a bunch of keys from the counter. "Will you go to the garage and get something easier to cook? A pizza or something."

"You're letting me drive your mid-life crisis-mobile?"

"I've been drinking."

Rachel rolled her eyes. "Okay. You wait here, Brian. Looks like daddy could use a hand with that wine."

Everybody Be Cool

John checked his scarf was tied tight around his face and pulled the peak of his baseball cap down low. Then he strolled into Murdock's garage with the revolver held by his side, pointed at the floor. The shop assistant was too busy doing something to her fingernails to notice him at first but she almost jumped out of her skin as John started screaming at the top of his lungs.

"Hey you! Get down. No, wait. Open the till. Stand back! Freeze."

"Fucking stick to one thing, will you? What do you want me to do?"

John maintained the same ear-battering volume. "Open the till. No funny business."

"Mister, I don't even get minimum wage in here. Just relax and I'll give you anything you want."

John lowered his voice. "Oh, dead on. Well, fill a plastic bag full of cash."

"Do you not want the cigarettes as well?"

"Aye. Good idea. Thanks."

She turned to swipe the fags off the shelves behind her and into the bag. John took the opportunity to watch her ass sway as she worked.

"You know," he said. "I'd love to ask you for your number."

"Probably not the best time."

"Aye, probably."

Wheels Man

Paul fidgeted in the driver seat of the stolen Vauxhall Astra. He tried to catch a glimpse of John through the glass automatic doors of Murdock's garage. The sunlight bounced off the doors' surface. Paul had no idea what the little scumbag was up to.

"Come on, John. What the fuck's keeping you?"

Paul's scalp tightened. The rear view mirror reflected the last thing he wanted to see: a police car pulled into the garage forecourt.

"Ah, fuck."

His hand hovered over the car horn.

"Ah, fuck."

He laid his hand on the plastic button in the centre of the steering wheel. Applied a little pressure then snatched his hand back.

"Fuck it."

He eased the stolen car into gear and drove coolly and calmly away from the garage.

Hands Up

John was well pleased with himself as he strutted out of the shop with his loot. Right up until he walked right into a peeler. He dropped one of his bags of cigarettes and the packets scattered all over the concrete.

The cop looked from John's still concealed face to the fags and back to John again. "You should seriously consider nicotine patches." He pointed at the fags. "They'll kill you."

John dropped the other bag and pushed his wrists forward to be cuffed. The cop snapped the silver bracelets in place. Just as he reached out to snatch the scarf from John's face, the screech of tyre on concrete snatched John's attention. A green Subaru Impreza pulled into the garage forecourt. John placed the vanity number plate right away. M47ONE. It was his da's car. Trust the aul' bastard to pick that instant to arrive. Just in time to gloat.

But it wasn't his da who jumped out of the Subaru. That would have been too easy. As soon as he spotted Rachel he knew he was in real trouble. She stormed across the forecourt and John could have sworn he could see twin plumes of steam spouting from her nose.

"John! What the fuck?"

The cop actually jumped at the urgent whip-crack that was Rachel's voice. Then he went back to frisking John. He found the revolver tucked in John's waistband immediately.

Rachel seethed. "A gun? A fucking gun? Where'd you get a gun from?"

The cop half-turned and tried to stare Rachel down. "He has the right to remain silent, you know."

Rachel looked over the cop's shoulder. John shifted to the cop's blind side and mouthed Paul's name. Rachel nodded. Understood.

"Will I tell daddy?" she asked.

"No. I'll phone my solicitor from the station."

"We've an expert here, have we?" the cop said.

"What are you, a comedian?" Rachel asked.

The cop gave Rachel a cool look.

"Go stand by your car, please, miss," he said. "I'll be over in a minute to check your tyres."

Male Bonding

Brian was warming to Rachel's father. They'd just emptied one bottle of wine and uncorked another. It was going down pretty damn easy, especially since Brian was normally a beer man. They weren't quite best friends, but they were getting there.

Brian checked his watch. "Rachel's taking a long time."

Malone curved one side of his mouth and spluttered a blast of wine-breath through his lips."Ah, she's probably got chatting to somebody she knows. Small towns are like that. We talk."

"I guess."

"You know, like, I've heard a few things about you and your brother."

"I don't suppose it was good?"

"Afraid not."

"Look, me and Paul..."

Malone held up his hand. It wavered slightly. "Don't. I'm not going to chase you out of my house."

"Really?"

"Nobody's perfect."

"That's very gracious."

"Besides. You might be able to do me a favour."

Burn

Paul pulled the stolen Astra into a parking space on the promenade. A raised flowerbed housing bushy shrubs and bushier weeds partly concealed it from the road leading in. Paul climbed out and had a quick glance around him. Nobody about. He took two cans of lighter fluid from his coat pocket and squirted them onto the cloth seats. Then he struck a match and touched it to the phosphorous tips of the other matches in the cardboard sleeve. The box flared and he tossed it into the car.

Paul stood at a safe distance for a few minutes to make sure the car – the evidence – caught alight. The old thrill he remembered from all those joyrides in his misspent youth scrabbled about in his chest. He left, unseen, before the windows and tyres started cracking and popping.

A Subtle Proposition

Brian felt a little overwhelmed as Malone ranted between gulps of wine. Lost even. So he did what he always did in moments of uncertainty. He said as little as possible.

"This recession is fucking with everybody, Brian. Construction has come to a standstill. The private sector is fucked. My timber yard's haemorrhaging money."

Brian nodded. "Hard times."

"Yeah, but there's a way you could help me out." Malone slurped another heroic mouthful of red wine from his goblet. Then he tipped Brian a conspiratorial wink. "You've a bit of a past, haven't you?"

Brian fought hard to keep the indignation from his voice. It was true after all. "What would you know about that?"

"Small towns, Brian. Remember?" He chuckled then quaffed half his goblet. "Anyway I think, between us, we could make this problem of mine go up in smoke."

Brian would never claim to be a genius, but he was able to decipher this less than subtle proposition. Still, he couldn't resist blurting: "Wait. You want me to torch the timber yard?"

Lam It

Paul barged into his house and bolted up the stairs. He dumped his clothes out of his wardrobe and onto his bed. He gathered the four corners of the blanket together and slung the whole kit and caboodle over his shoulder. He blundered back down the stairs and stood in the living room. Took a moment. Breathed. Thought.

Then he whipped his mobile from his hip pocket and tapped out a text message.

Something's Up

Brian's phone bleeped and broke the stretched silence between him and his girlfriend's father. He called up a new text message and skimmed over it.

"Anything important?" Malone asked.

Brian put his phone down on the tabletop. "Just my brother. I'll get back to him."

Malone took a gulp from his wine glass and topped it up from a fresh bottle. "So, the timber yard. What do you think? If you don't want to do it, we could ask Paul, couldn't we?"

Brian rubbed his stomach. He fixed his gaze on the wine glass. Opened his mouth to talk.

"Hi, boys."

Brian and Malone jolted in their seats. They turned to find Rachel standing in the doorway. She killed the conversation dead. Brian could have leapt out of his seat and kissed her. But he played it cool.

"Behaving yourselves?" she asked.

Malone spoke up. "Just getting to know your friend, here."

Rachel nodded then sighed. "That's nice."

"Did you not get the pizza?" Malone asked.

"What? Oh, no. They... They were all out of pizza. I'll just throw some sandwiches together."

Rachel moved to the fridge, slump-shouldered.

"Everything okay, babe?" Brian asked.

"Yeah."

Brian knew she was lying. Malone didn't seem to notice or mind. He just poured another glass.

I Want YOU!

Paul paced the room. His blanket tote-sack of possessions sat on the sofa, ready to go. He checked then rechecked his phone.

Then it rang.

O'Rourke calling.

"Ach, shite."

He glared at the screen for a couple of rings. Squinted and scowled as if he could change the caller ID by willpower. Then he gave in and answered it. "Hello?"

O'Rourke's voice rasped in his ear.

"Paul. Come to my office."

"Sure, no problem, man."

"And bring the gun."

"The gun? Already? Jesus, I only just got it."

"Something's come up. Get here quick."

O'Rourke cut the call. Paul grabbed the blanket tote-bag off the sofa and threw it at the wall. His bundled possessions scattered about the room. He kicked at them and almost slipped on a pair of silk boxers. Panic swelled in his stomach and a scream clawed its way up the lining of his throat.

"JESUS!"

Panic Stations

Brian sat in the passenger seat of Malone's Subaru and noted how confidently Rachel handled the beast of an engine. It was a welcome distraction to watch her skinny-jean encased legs pump the pedals as she shifted gears and worked the accelerator. He clutched a bottle of wine by the neck and squeezed tight as she barrelled around a big corner.

"You're very quiet," Rachel said. "You all right?"

Brian squinted at her. "So are you. What's wrong?"

"I asked first."

"I'm just thinking."

Rachel gave him a look but said nothing. They pulled up to Brian's house a few minutes later.

Brian laid a hand on Rachel's thigh. "Coming in for a cuppa or something, babe?"

"Sure." She paused for a second then asked: "Think your Paul will be there?"

"Aye. Too early for him to be out causing trouble."

"Oh, I'd say he could cause trouble any time of the day."

Brian led Rachel into the living room. Paul leapt off the sofa and was on him like fly on a turd.

"Where the fuck have you been, wee bro?"

"Out. What's your problem?"

"I'm in the shit, Brian."

"Have you seen our John today?" Rachel asked.

Paul's attention was diverted by Rachel's question and Brian took the opportunity to scoot past his brother and make his way towards the kitchen.

"I'll put the kettle on," Brian said.

Paul grabbed him by the elbow and stopped Brian in his tracks.

"No, don't. We have to get out of here, wee bro."

Brian rubbed his flip-flopping stomach. "What did you do?"

"I'll tell you about it on the way out of here. Just get your shit together, okay?"

Rachel jumped in. "You can't expect him to drop everything and run. He has a life here now, you know?"

"A life here?" Paul tilted his head and gave Rachel a look. "Tell me once and for all, are you pregnant or what?"

Rachel sat on the sofa. She breathed slowly. Brian immediately recognised it as her calming exercise; the one that never really worked. She was fit to blow and he couldn't think of a way to prevent it and, in truth, he wasn't all that sure he wanted to prevent it.

She spoke in a soft and measured tone. "Don't be a prick, Paul."

Brian shouldered past Paul to join Rachel on the couch.

"You've some explaining to do, big bro."

Snuffing Charlie

O'Rourke tilted back his leather chair. It creaked under his weight, but he knew it would hold. Had paid enough to make sure it could support him. Charlie was back in the visitor's chair, tied up again and only a little less bloody. Owen, one of O'Rourke's employees, stood at the door.

"We going to top this piece of shite or what?" Owen asked.

O'Rourke consulted his watch. The young Belfast lad was taking the piss. He should have been at the office 10 minutes after O'Rourke had summoned him. Everywhere in The Point was within 10 minutes of O'Rourke's office. Maybe Paul wanted to make a statement. Put across that he wouldn't answer to every beck and call. As much as he liked the youngster, O'Rourke would have to beat that out of him. Right after the fucker did the job he'd been called to do.

"No. We'll wait another half hour for Paul. When he does the deed, he's really one of us. Charlie's not going anywhere, are you, son?"

Shit Magnet

Brian's head went from side to side as he tracked Paul's frantic pacing up and down the living room. It bugged the shit out of him, but he didn't want to go off on a meaningless tangent. He bit his tongue and waited for Paul to continue his confession.

Rachel wasn't as patient.

She prompted Paul. "And you did *what* with the gun?"

"I tossed it off the end of the pier."

Brian thought he heard Rachel mumble something under her breath, possibly "bullshit," but he ignored it for the sake of momentum and offered his own prompt instead.

"Why do something as stupid as ask for a gun and then toss it two minutes later?"

"I freaked out, okay? I asked for the gun on a whim. When I actually got it, it scared me to death."

"Why not just give it back to O'Rourke, then?" Rachel asked.

"And look like a pussy? What are you, nuts?"

"I'm not the buck-eejit in trouble with a gangster."

"Yes, okay. We've established that I've messed up. Now can we get going before I *get* messed up?"

Rachel took a deep breath. Brian was quite impressed by her composure. He didn't know why, but her subdued mood from earlier seemed to have seeped into her reactions towards Paul's major stupidity. Maybe this was just her way in a crisis. If so, Brian had nothing but admiration for her.

"You know what you could do, Paul?" Rachel said.

"What?"

"Go to O'Rourke and tell him you had to get rid of the gun because you were being followed by a cop. You thought they were going to search you for drugs so you got rid of everything."

Brian nodded. "That sounds pretty reasonable, big bro. Do that."

Paul shook his head. "No. O'Rourke's not reasonable. In fact, he's a fucking nutcase. He'll not accept that. We just have to get out of here."

"I don't see why this has to be a 'we' situation," Rachel said. "Brian's not in trouble."

"Oh, yeah? And you think O'Rourke won't pick him up and beat him with beer tins until he tells him where I've gone?"

Brian crimped his face. "Beer tins?"

Rachel growled a little. "God, you are a shit magnet, Paul Morgan."

More Shit

Mad Mickey quashed his munchies with a big bag of chips from the chip-van on Warrenpoint's town square. Dave chomped on a chicken burger. He'd gone local and asked for lashings of coleslaw in the burger. Mad Mickey thought he was a bit... well, mad. Mad Mickey took a deep breath and the vinegary chips mingled with the salt air. He looked out at the water. A big trawler was slowing to a stop in the docks.

"Nice place, isn't it?"

Dave nodded and swallowed a lump of chicken breast and coleslaw. "Lovely, boss."

"Not too big either, is it?"

Dave considered this for a second. "Nope."

"Shouldn't be too hard to find that Paul fellah, then, should it?"

"You wouldn't think so..."

"Then why have we been here for three days looking for him?"

"Just bad luck I suppose." Dave bit off another chunk of his burger. He spoke with his mouth full. "There's a bright side, though."

"What's that?"

"Fresh air, chips, ice cream. I haven't had a wee break like this for years. It's nice."

"Nice?" Mad Mickey spat pieces of chewed-up chip as he shouted. "Fucking nice?"

A couple of passing old biddies gasped at the sudden outburst.

Dave swallowed again. "Aye. Nice."

Mad Mickey plucked a spliff from out of his dreads. He lit it and sucked down a huge draw. He wheezed a little as he exhaled.

"Actually, it *is* nice. But don't you get too relaxed. We've work to do."

Scummy by Association

Brian got up off the sofa and laid a hand on Paul's chest to stop his pacing. Rachel followed his lead and stood at his side, facing Paul. He thought she was worried him and Paul might kick off, but that wasn't Brian's style. Yes, his mind thrummed with bottled-up anger, but he wasn't going to scuffle with Paul. He knew Paul would beat seven shades out of him if he tried. But he couldn't continue to do nothing. To bite his lip. So he opened his mouth and just let the words flow.

"You know, I came here because you thought it would be a good idea, Paul. I had my doubts, but look how things turned out. I settled in nicely. Got a job, a girl, didn't have to break into houses for money. It felt pretty good. But then you took me to the Chinese. And after that, you beat up Rachel's ex. But I figured, that's Paul. He'll always be in trouble. I can rise above. But I was wrong about that. Of course, I can't rise above."

"Bro, time's getting on."

"I'm trying to make a point here, Paul."

Paul threw his hands up, but restrained his tongue. Brian continued: "Thing is, bro, I'll never be happy if I let you drag me down, will I? Brother or not, you'll fuck up my life. And I think you know it. You just don't care enough to want to stop yourself."

"I don't care enough? Come on, wee bro. You're breaking my heart..."

"No, Paul. Just stop it. You can't talk me around this time. I'm staying here. It's time for you to move on, not me."

Rachel tugged at Brian's sleeve. "Brian, as much as I agree with you, you can't stay here right now. Paul's right. They'll use you to get to him."

Brian felt himself sag. He'd taken a stand against Paul. Wrestled for control of his own life, and for nothing. It was out of reach.

"Come on," Paul said. "We've wasted ages now. We need to move. Can we take your da's car, Rachel?"

"No you cannot!" Rachel folded her arms and cocked her hips. "We could probably use our John's though, couldn't we?"

"What 'we' is this?" Brian asked. "Me, you and Paul?"

Rachel ignored the question and Brian felt as if control had moved another step out of his grasp.

"I think John's going away for a while," Rachel said. "He must have mentioned it to you, Paul. You two are as thick as thieves."

"He might have mentioned something, aye."

Rachel clapped her hands like a *maître d'* summoning the underlings. "Get your gear together, Brian. I'll take Paul down the road and we can stop off at mine. I'll put a bag together too. We'll be out of here in about 20 minutes. Be ready, okay?"

Brian wanted to argue, try and offer even a little resistance just for the sake of pride. But he knew it would only be a waste of time. So, he zipped it and headed off to gather his shit together.

Pain in the Neck

O'Rourke slammed his palm down on the mahogany desk. Charlie jerked and whimpered. O'Rourke hauled himself out of his leather office chair, stalked across the room and unloaded a right cross into Charlie's face. Owen, hardened thug or not, flinched as Charlie's head snapped back. O'Rourke remained in front of Charlie until he could raise his beaten head again. He gurgled blood as O'Rourke cupped his chin in his hand.

"Paul's let me down, Charlie," O'Rourke said. "So, I'll just take care of you myself. Nighty-night."

O'Rourke grabbed Charlie's head in his hands and twisted it to the right with a grunt. Charlie's neck cracked. O'Rourke backed away and Charlie's head lolled forward.

O'Rourke turned to Owen. "Go get Paul and bring him here. I should never have given that sneaky Belfast shite a chance."

He went back to his desk and scribbled on a scrap of paper.

"That's his address, okay?"

Owen nodded and left.

Where Can I Drop You?

Rachel turned right at the painted-on roundabout at the bottom of Duke Street. The Subaru's engine grumbled. Invited her to feed it more juice. But she took it easy. She needed to buy a little time and figure out what to do about her passenger. Paul fiddled with the radio. Rachel slapped his hand away from the knobs and buttons.

Paul snapped his hand back. "Hey! No need for that."

She was done with the pussyfooting. "Did you give John the gun?"

"How do you know about the gun?"

"Did you give it to him?"

"I didn't force it on him. He asked me for the thing. It's not my fault he got lifted."

"And I suppose it's not your fault that Brian's the way he is?"

"What's that supposed to mean? There's nothing wrong with Brian."

"There's less wrong with him now, but he's been your doormat for years."

"Aye, says you who's known him five minutes." Paul tilted his head slightly, looked beyond Rachel and out the driver-side window. "SHITE!"

Rachel jerked in her seat. The Subaru swerved slightly. She righted their course as her heart vibrated.

"What?" she asked.

Paul pointed out the window. "Mad Mickey. Jesus, what's he doing here?"

Rachel followed Paul's line of sight and looked out her window. A crusty white hippy in green fatigues and a big gorilla-type in a suit loitered outside the Country Fried Chicken. They checked out passers-by in a less than subtle manner and generally looked menacing. Rachel felt a sly smile spread across her face. She pushed in the cigarette lighter.

"Why are you slowing down?" Paul asked. "They'll see us."

"No they won't."

She rapped her knuckles on the window.

Tinted.

Rachel stopped the car and reached into the backseat.

"What are you doing? Drive."

She patted her hand along the leather seat then reached down into the foot well. *There*. Her hand wrapped around the cool steel of the steering wheel lock her daddy had bought but rarely used.

"Wait just a second," Rachel said.

"For what?"

The cigarette lighter popped. Paul looked to it then Rachel; tried to figure things out. With her free hand, Rachel snatched the lighter from its socket and shoved it into the side of Paul's neck. He screamed. She hefted the steering wheel lock. Working in the confined space, she butted him with a spear-like jab. His eyes rolled back and his neck went rubbery. Rachel reached across his lap and pulled the passenger door handle. She shoved him out onto the kerb then leant on the horn.

Across the street, the hippy and the big guy zeroed in on the source of the blaring noise. Rachel wound down her tinted window, waved at the two men and drove forward a few yards to reveal Paul as he struggled to get to his feet.

"There he is!" The hippy's gravely voice was loud and excitable. "Come on!"

He sprinted towards Paul, closely followed by the big man in the suit. Rachel whooped as she sank her toes down on the pedal and peeled off down the street.

Unwelcome Guest

Brian dropped a bulging canvas bag on the living room floor. It thwacked off the laminate flooring and sent fluffy balls of dust skittering in all directions. He regarded the bag for a second, unimpressed. All his worldly possessions, jammed into such a small space.

Brian's head snapped up at the sound of tyres screeching at the front of the house. He went to the window. A car had skidded to a halt and come to rest broad side at the mouth of Brian's driveway. A burly skinhead clambered out of the car. He consulted a small piece of paper, squinted at the number on Brian's door and ran towards the house. Brian gasped as the skinhead barrelled into the front door. The wooden doorframe creaked and cracked. Another thump and wood splintered. Brian ran to the kitchen.

Brian grappled with the back door handle. The door held solid.

"Where the fuck's the key?"

He spotted it, hanging on a hook on the wall. Paul's idea. Nobody's more security conscious than a burglar. Brian lunged for it. Fumbled. Cursed as it fell. All the while the booming at the front door continued. Brian scooped up the keys. The front door gave. Bounced off the wall.

The skinhead stormed in.

He tramped through the living room and spotted Brian in the kitchen through the open dividing door. Brian looked to the knife block on the kitchen counter. Five good blades, only a little out of grasp. He reached out, could have had them drawn and ready. But he shook his head. He couldn't *stab* somebody. No way. He was not a killer.

"O'Rourke wants to see Paul," the skinhead said.

"You couldn't have knocked?" Brian asked. "Phoned maybe?"

"O'Rourke is a serious man. He calls you once. After that, I arrive." He rolled his big shiny head on his thick muscled neck. "So, where is he?"

"Out."

The skinhead pulled back his jacket to reveal a chrome pistol in a shoulder holster.

"I hope your next answer's a little better." He let go of his jacket and it fell back into place. "When's he back?"

"Soon."

"That's a little better." He smiled at Brian. "You going to put the kettle on?"

Brian flicked on the already full kettle. The skinhead continued to smile and unnerve the hell out of Brian.

"What did he do wrong?" Brian asked, desperate to get the skinhead talking and wipe away his seemingly friendly grin.

"Not for me to say."

Brian nodded. "Fair enough. Probably better I don't know anyway. Milk and sugar?"

"Just milk."

"Sweet enough, are you?"

"Fucking fruit, are you?"

And Brian felt a little bit better. You knew where you stood with an attitude like that.

The skinhead had stationed himself in front of the fridge. Brian went to gently nudge the guy aside. He slapped Brian's arm away aggressively. The force of the slap twisted Brian at the waist and he threw out his other arm in search of a steadying force. His hand landed on the skinhead. Slipped inside his jacket. A pickpocket instinct took over and Brian snagged the skinhead's pistol. He stepped back and raised the gun.

The heft of the pistol sent a surge of power through Brian's core. But, even armed and dangerous, he couldn't keep the nerves out of his voice. "I was just trying to get the milk, you dickhead."

Here Comes Trouble

O'Rourke stared across his desk at Charlie's slumped corpse. The dead weakling sickened him. He'd left behind a wife and a kid because he couldn't manage his gambling. Fucking loser. The world was a better place without him.

He checked his watch and considered calling Owen to see if he'd caught up with Paul. Then he heard the clatter of hurried footsteps and yelling. The commotion came from the yard in front of his building. His front door opened. The footsteps sounded in his corridor. Then Paul burst into the office, screaming with his hands in the air.

"Richard, Richard!" Paul said. "Watch out. They're trying to pull a move on you."

"What?"

"No time. They're coming!"

O'Rourke jumped to his feet and flipped his big office desk on its side. Paul scrabbled around the makeshift cover and hunched down beside O'Rourke.

O'Rourke ripped the Velcro-fastened sawn-off shotgun from the underside of his desk. He pumped it then turned to Paul. Noticed fresh facial wounds and a nasty burn on the side of his neck. He grabbed Paul's upper arm.

"Who is it?" O'Rourke asked. "The Newry crew?"

"Don't know. They grabbed me off the street earlier. Tried to get me to lead them to you."

"Well you've done that now, haven't you?"

"But only so I could warn you. Anybody else would have left you to get fucked."

The rumble of feet pounding linoleum filled the corridor again. A big yeti in a suit entered noisily. O'Rourke stood up and emptied both barrels. The yeti took one in the chest and one in the face. He went down. Revealed a blood-spattered Woodstock reject. The hippy howled and raised a huge automatic pistol.

He unloaded half a clip. The rounds slammed into the reinforced desktop. O'Rourke, hunkered down and shielded, reloaded his sawn-off.

Warning Shot

Brian held the skinhead at gunpoint. The skinhead took a step forward. Brian thumbed back the hammer. The skinhead halted.

"That's right," Brian said. "I've seen plenty of movies. I know how to work these things. Now, step back."

"You won't shoot, though."

Brian's silence was taken as an affirmation of the skinhead's statement. He took another step forward. Brian jerked backwards. Just wanted a little space. But his sudden movement set the gun off. A good chunk of the skinhead's ear vaporised. He cupped it with both hands and screamed. Blood seeped through his fingers.

Little black specks floated in Brian's vision. His knees shook. He bit the inside of his cheek to keep himself in the moment. "Uh, that was a warning shot," he said.

The skinhead's eyes popped wide open. They rolled like cue balls. "Warning? You fucking hit me!"

"I was aiming for above your head. Sorry."

"I'll kill you!"

"You sure you want another warning?"

The skinhead shut his eyes. "No. Please don't."

Brian thumbed back the hammer again. "Back up. Into the living room."

He left the skinhead standing in the corner, gagged and bound with socks and Xbox leads.

Out on the street Brian stood by the skinhead's car with his phone to his ear. "Come on. Answer." But it rang off. "Bastard!"

Brian pocketed the phone and jumped into the car. He gunned the engine. The valves and cylinders whined in tuned-up ecstasy. Brian set the pistol on the passenger seat and peeled out onto the street, then onto the main road into Warrenpoint.

Last Stand

Paul cowered behind the desk and prayed O'Rourke would save him. Mad Mickey used the wall dividing the corridor and the office as cover. O'Rourke bounced up and emptied both barrels. Paul heard thuds and sharp cracks as the cartridges knocked lumps out of the door frame. Mad Mickey coughed. The sound of a lighter flint sparking cut across the smoky room. Paul couldn't smell it above the choking stink of cordite but knew that Mad Mickey had just blazed a spliff. The mad bastard. Then five bullets battered the table and the wall behind it. Plaster dust fell like fine snow. Paul's ears rang.

O'Rourke shook Paul to get his attention then mouthed: "Get your gun out."

Paul hissed back. "I haven't got it."

"Where is it?"

Paul could just about hear O'Rourke over the diminishing ring in his ear.

"They took it when they lifted me."

"Who the fuck are they?"

Paul shook his head. "No idea."

Mad Mickey coughed. "Ah, come on, now, Paul. Tell the man who I am."

O'Rourke glared at Paul. "How does he know...?"

"I told him when he was beating me."

Mad Mickey snorted and wheezed. "I didn't need to beat you for that." He sighed. "Mister new boss. I'm the old boss and that wee bastard owes me a van and a pound of flesh. Just send the fucker out to me and I'll leave peacefully."

"He's lying, Richard," Paul said. "Don't listen to him."

"Well, I've nothing to lose by sending you out. Sorry, son. But you're expendable. I'm not."

O'Rourke pushed Paul out from the cover of the table. Paul screamed an incoherent protest. Mad Mickey sniggered. He stepped into the office and trained the automatic on Paul. Paul raised his hands. O'Rourke stood and blind-sided Mad Mickey. The hippy-gangster took one in the ribs. He went down. Paul loosed an animalistic sob.

"Sorry, Paul," O'Rourke said. "I had to make it seem real."

Paul wiped his running nose with his sleeve. "Jesus. You're some actor, mate. You had me convinced." He got his breathing under control and thought about standing. "Bit of a risky move, don't you think?"

"It was a calculated risk," O'Rourke said.

"Aye?"

"Yeah, I took myself out of the equation."

More shots rang out.

O'Rourke's bulk slammed against the wall. He slid down it, leaving a bloody trail. Paul turned to see Mad

Mickey lying down, his gun raised in the air. He wheeled it on Paul.

"Fucking math-humour," Mad Mickey said. "Unforgiveable."

Blood foamed on the hippy-gangster's lips as he cracked a smile.

"Mickey, please. Don't. Let it go."

"Let it go? You got me fucking killed."

Mad Mickey pulled the trigger. It clicked. Empty. His gun hand fell to the floor. He breathed shallowly. Paul went to O'Rourke's body and wrestled the shotgun from his death grip. Mad Mickey slowly fumbled in his pocket. Tried to snag a clip. His hand came away with one, but it was too late. Paul put him out of his misery.

He wiped his prints off the sawn-off with the tail of his shirt and dropped it by O'Rourke's side. Thought maybe he could remove himself from the equation. He stepped out the door, stopped and went back for Mad Mickey's gun and clip. It'd fuck with the crime scene and hint at another person's presence, but fuck it. The way his day was going he couldn't risk going without protection. He slammed the clip home before leaving.

Hit and Run

Rachel watched Paul from her daddy's car as he walked out onto the street. He didn't look both ways. She cranked the Subaru into first and sank the toe. Paul didn't see her coming. He was flipped into the air, landed on the bonnet and slid down onto the road. Rachel opened the car door and stepped out. Another car screeched to a stop at the scene. Rachel glanced over at it and saw Brian behind the wheel. He got out. Staggered to the front of the Subaru.

"Jesus Christ, Rachel! What the fuck did you do?"

Rachel tried to wing it. Lied her ass off. "It was an accident! I was coming back here from my place to meet him. All my stuff's in the car."

"Shit, shit, shit, shit, shit. Why wasn't he with you?"

"He'd gone to O'Rourke's office to try and get some money. He thought there was a chance the big man would be out looking for him."

Brian howled like a dying dog. "Stupid bastard." Fat tears rolled down his cheeks. "Is he dead?"

Rachel looked down at Paul. It didn't bode well for him. He was bent in places that shouldn't bend. "I don't know." She spotted something in Brian's hand. "What's that, Brian?"

Brian held up a revolver. "He was right. Somebody came looking for him. He's still at ours. Probably bleeding to death as we speak."

"You shot him?"

Brian nodded. "Took off his ear."

"It probably wasn't fatal." She looked her boyfriend up and down. He did not look well. "Why don't you give me the gun, Brian? You're upset."

Brian's tear-filled eyes fell to the heap of broken bones in front of the Subaru. His mouth formed an 'O' and his whole body tensed. Rachel froze, sure Brian was about to shoot her. He dove at her. A fraction of a second later a gunshot boomed. Rachel and Brian landed in a heap. Paul groaned and gurgled. He was fucked but still alive, armed and dangerous.

The car provided a little cover from Paul. Brian had dropped the pistol when they hit the tarmac. Rachel reached for it. The Subaru rocked on its suspension. Paul cursed. He was trying to get to her. Rachel stretched another inch and snagged the pistol grip. She fumbled with the gun then slipped a finger into the trigger guard. Paul dragged himself around the car. He raised his gun.

Brian's voice cracked. "Paul, please don't. I love her."

Paul hesitated for a split second. Showed a little love for his wee bro for once.

Rachel shot him in the head.

Brian loosed a stomach-curdling scream.

Off Into the Sunset

Brian sat silently in the passenger seat. Rachel drove. Everything seemed kind of insulated and he wondered if he was in shock. Rachel had set the pistol on the dashboard. The instrument of death that had caved in Paul's face. Brian shivered but maintained an odd sense of equilibrium. It wasn't all right that Paul had died. Not at all. And it certainly was not cool that Rachel had murdered him. But he didn't freak out. Just felt kind of... numb.

Rachel took a hard right and the gun slid across the dash. It landed in Brian's lap. He sensed Rachel tense.

She sounded nervous and wary as she spoke. "We had to do it, Brian. It was him or us. You get that, don't you?"

"*We?*"

Rachel reached out for the gun in Brian's lap. He laid both of his hands over it. Shook his head. He didn't make eye contact with Rachel.

"Just drive," he said.

"Where to?"

Brian shrugged, ever so slightly. "Doesn't matter. Just drive."

Rachel nodded. Sirens sounded in the distance. Brian watched her check the rear view mirror. She didn't panic and he guessed they were in the clear. Temporarily, at least. Rachel eyed the gun in Brian's lap again. He curled a hand around the grip. Thumbed back the hammer then eased it into place again. Rachel swallowed. She returned her attention to the road ahead.

They drove towards the sunset.

THE END

Acknowledgements

For their constant support, patience and love I thank my wife, Michelle, and our kids, Mya, Jack and Oscar. You guys keep me on the straight and narrow and I don't even begrudge you for it.

So that they don't give me grief at dinner on Sunday, thanks to my parents, Joe and Rosemary, and my siblings, Lisa, Mark and Tanya.

Mike Stone, my good friend and most respected reader/editor/problem-shooter, you're worth your weight in gold, mate.

Danny and the guys at Pulp Press, thank you for taking a chance on this wee story.

A shout-out to the Irish crime fiction community: Much respect to the Godfathers, Colin Bateman and Ken Bruen. Keep on truckin', David Torrans and the staff at No Alibis Bookstore in Belfast, a national treasure; I can't thank you enough.

For inspiration and encouragement, thanks to the new NI crime fiction generation, Adrian McKinty, Stuart Neville and Brian McGilloway. A tonne of gratitude for Ian Sansom, a saint and scholar of the highest order. And, of course, Arlene Hunt...you rock.

Special thanks to Declan Burke, the most energetic supporter and top shelf writer of 'Emerald Noir'.

The list could go on but I really have to wrap this up.